Twin Rivers

When Clay Westbrook, a cowhand on a Wyoming ranch in the 1890s, sticks up for a Mexican sheepherder, he runs into serious trouble.

But Clay maintains his friendship with the Mexicans, much to the dislike of the bullying rancher Sutton and his gang of thugs. He even develops an ill-advised romantic interest in Tony's niece, Guadalupe.

Before long, Clay finds himself without a job and is harassed by Sutton and his men, who burn down his homesteader's shack and sabotage his outfitting camp. Clay then discovers that Sutton has designs on his homestead and plans to cut a ditch project across the land. It is up to Clay to thwart Sutton . . . but can he do so in time?

Twin Rivers

John D. Nesbitt

A Black Horse Western

ROBERT HALE · LONDON

© John D. Nesbitt 1995
First published 1995
This edition published in Great Britain 2010

ISBN 978-0-7090-9001-4

Robert Hale Limited
Clerkenwell House
Clerkenwell Green
London EC1R 0HT

www.halebooks.com

Typeset by
Derek Doyle & Associates, Shaw Heath
Printed and bound in Great Britain by
CPI Antony Rowe, Chippenham and Eastbourne

CHAPTER 1

Clay Westbrook gave his horse loose rein until they reached the top of the bluff overlooking the river. Then he turned the horse and stopped to take in a full view of the scene below.

At this point in its course, the river forked to flow around the sides of a diamond-shaped island. From down at the river's edge a person could not clearly see the two forks diverging and coming together. But from the hilltop, Clay could see the island, forty acres of grass and trees, emerald green in the late spring sun, looking calm as the current rippled on both sides.

Early Indians must have viewed this place from this lookout, he thought, when they decided to call it Twin Rivers. That would have been long before there was a town here, when the area was just a place for people to stop and stay awhile. Old tepee rings showed where the Indians in their yearly wandering had camped on the safe, high spots along the river.

Trappers, too, had favored this spot. They were probably the ones who cut what were now old notches in the cottonwoods on both sides of the river, half a mile upstream, to mark the ford. Clay could imagine the trappers camped on the riverbank, moving upstream with their traps and downstream with their bundles of furs. The trappers, who had picked up a wealth of habits and phrases from the Indians, had also called this place Twin Rivers.

Behind Clay to the north, as he sat on his horse and watched the river, lay the town of Greenfield. Less than ten years earlier, a group of settlers established the town and laid out a plan of streets, imposing their geometric order over a place that earlier people had left unbothered. They named it Greenfield after a town in Illinois where several of them came from. Although he had his back to the town, Clay had a sense of its presence. The name seemed misplaced, especially at times like this when the

5

world seemed magical, a place where a sparkling river wrapped its legs around an island.

Clay looked off to the west, where a winding cord of bluffs and trees marked the course of the river. The river flowed toward him, from west to east. Clay knew where the smaller streams fed into it – Stone Creek, Saddle Creek, Cedar Creek, and so forth. The broad slant of the plains on either side of the river was a treeless sea of grass. Travelers and range riders usually looked for areas that had a string of trees, assuming they held the promise, not always fulfilled, of water.

From where he watched, Clay could see Saddle Creek flowing into the river, a full six miles to the southwest. Four miles up that stream was the spot where Clay had picked a site for a homestead. It was only a hundred and sixty acres, nowhere near enough to make a living with his own cattle, but it would be a place to call his own. He had ridden hard to Cheyenne, two days each way, to file a claim with the U.S. Land Office. That had been a month earlier, and today was the first chance he had gotten to ride out here. He worked as a cowboy for the Cross Pole Ranch; like the other ranch hands, he bunked at headquarters about seventeen miles northwest of town.

As Clay looked across the plains that spread out all around him, he thought the land looked as it always had, but he knew it was changing. The days of the open range were coming to an end. Up close, a man could ride the range for days and not know the difference, but then he would come to a fence or a train track, a line of steel that cut the land into pieces. First it had been the railroad, with its iron roosters trailing plumes of smoke. It had cut across the south of Wyoming on the first big run, and then new lines had come north and west into the cow country. The trains had brought nesters with barbed wire, plows, and more lately, windmills. Clay had heard that the next to come would be the big ditch projects, which promised to bring water to those homesteaders not fortunate enough to take up land next to streams.

He nodded slowly. Even if he couldn't see the changes from up here, he knew Wyoming was changing. People and tools and instruments were moving west just as sure as the river was flowing east. The country wasn't going fast, but it was going, and if a fellow wanted to live here he'd best stake out his piece of it. It might even be better for the little man. Just a few years back, when it was all open range and only big outfits – and no sheep – a cowhand couldn't own his own cattle. Big outfits had not allowed a hired man to have his own cattle because he might put his brand on slicks, or calves that hadn't been branded. Now it was becoming more possible for a man to have his own stock, and that's what Clay hoped to do on his little spread of land up the second creek to the southwest. He'd like to have his own cattle, and a place to call home.

The sun was warm on Clay's left side – warm on the denim jacket he wore and on the saddle leather his leg lay against. He leaned forward and patted the warm shiny neck of his horse, and he took in the healthy smell of the fresh air. As the sun came on stronger in the spring, it seemed to liven the air. Clay patted the horse again, enjoying the rich sorrel color, the warmth to his hand, the scent of the animal. A meadowlark tinkled its five notes. Clay sat up in the saddle and listened, waiting to hear the song again.

He heard instead the cry of the iron rooster, behind him to the east. The westbound train hooted again, chugging along the track that ran parallel to the river. Clay winced. Then he looked again to the southwest, to the place where his hundred and sixty acres were, even though it was not visible from here, and he smiled. Next he reined his horse around and rode down the back side of the bluff.

As he sidehilled down to the base of the bluff, he thought it would be a good time to let the sorrel, Rusty, have a drink. He knew of a spot a quarter of a mile upstream, before the ford, where the land sloped down to the river's edge and made a good spot for watering animals.

At the bottom of the bluff he turned his horse to head west, then stopped. A magpie had changed its course in midflight, and he looked around to see why. Two riders were coming up out of a swale, headed for the spot Clay had in mind. They had already ridden past him, apparently without seeing him, but he got a good look at them. Theodore Sutton and Alex Thode were no great friends of Clay, so he decided to give them plenty of time to pass.

Sutton was easily recognizable: a big man who rode a big bay horse. As owner of the Silver Plains Land and Cattle Company south of the river, he had plenty of horses to ride, but when he rode into town it was usually on the long-legged bay, which must have stood seventeen hands. Sutton did not have the lean, hard build that most cowpunchers had, but he was known as a good rider.

To Sutton's left rode his tagalong, Alex Thode. The crown of his hat was below the brim of Sutton's, but he was not a small man. He was square-built and muscular, about average height, and he rode a palomino that went about fifteen hands. Thode usually wore a leather vest, as he did now, and he was known for always wearing a clean shirt, which also looked to be the case today. He was the son of a Chicago banker, and Sutton had met him there after shipping a load of cattle. It was said that Thode had his own room in Sutton's ranch house and that he took a bath every day. He was not much of a range hand, but he fancied himself quite a roper and reportedly spent quite a bit of time practicing. He liked to rope against the cowboys, picking a small part of what he would see as their game, and trying to beat them at it. Clay had also heard that Thode was a good aim with a shotgun and had brought to the ranch some of the medals he had won at his father's shooting club.

Neither Sutton nor Thode was much to Clay's taste, and he was glad to have seen them first and let them go by. He imagined they would turn at the river and head upstream to the ford, so he gave them a long five minutes' lead before he pointed his horse toward the water.

As he waited, Clay remembered an incident from just the evening before, when he was in town. A man he barely knew, a straw boss or lesser foreman for the Silver Plains outfit, relayed an offer from Sutton. Clay could go to work for the big outfit, for ten dollars a month more than he was making at the Cross Pole. When Clay asked why Sutton didn't make the offer himself, the man said his boss was 'awful busy' but would give him a month to think it over. Since Clay didn't really know Sutton – had never met him – he'd thanked the man, said he'd think about it, then more or less forgot about it. Now, as Clay sat in his saddle in the warm sunlight, he reasoned that Sutton had probably been in town at the time, had some reason for wanting to hire him on,

8

but didn't consider him important enough to approach in person. Clay shook his head and moved his horse forward.

The small dips and rises of the land made it possible for a person to ride on to a scene without much warning, and that is what Clay did. Not fifty yards ahead of him was a straw-hatted Mexican sheepherder, on foot, with a flock of about twenty sheep that he had apparently been grazing toward water. It was a small herd of ewes and lambs. Facing the man, with their backs toward Clay, were the looming figures of Sutton and Thode.

Clay did not care for sheep, naturally, being a cowhand, but the land they were on was public domain, and the sheepherder had a right to be there. From the general look of things, however, it seemed as if Sutton and Thode wanted to interfere with that right. As Clay moved his horse nearer he caught a few of Sutton's words on the clear air.

'. . . like to run every damn one of 'em out of the country.'

Thode said something that Clay couldn't catch, and then Sutton said, 'I'd like that even better.'

Clay decided to let his horse walk right up to them rather than make it seem he was spying. The other two horsemen turned at the sound of horse hoofs on short grass. As they turned, Clay looked at the man on foot. It was Tony Campos, a man Clay had never met but knew by reputation to be a hard worker. He worked long hours at the stockyards, raised and sold vegetables in the summer, and kept a few head of sheep and goats. Tony did not show, by the look on his face, whether he expected help or more hazing. Clay tossed his head back a quarter of an inch by way of greeting, then looked at Sutton.

The big man, turning to look over his left shoulder, had untied his rope and held it against his right leg. Then he spoke, his voice barking across the clear air. 'You'd best stay out of this, cowboy.'

Clay didn't like to be ordered, but he said, 'Just passin' by.' He was pretty sure Sutton didn't recognize him or even know him by sight. Clay didn't mind leaving things that way.

Thode spoke up. 'I recommend you go around,' he said, pointing in a southwesterly direction toward the ford.

Clay nodded and turned his horse so that it angled toward the river instead of heading straight for it. He told himself it was none of his business and he rode on, without looking back.

Then he heard a slapping sound, and he turned to see Sutton jerking the loose end of his rope back to his right hand. Sutton swung out a wide loop, nudged his big horse forward, and slapped the loop against Campos, who jumped as the rope swatted him.

Something flared inside of Clay like the popping of a match. His teeth clenched and his right hand made a fist as he turned his horse around.

Sutton shook out his loop again, twirled it, and smacked the man who was on the ground. Campos flinched but stood game, facing Sutton and the horse straight on.

Thode was now moving around in back of Campos. In his movement was the message that he and Sutton were not going to let up on Clay's account. Thode had taken down his own rope by now, and it was apparent that he intended to rope Campos's feet.

Clay brought his horse within ten yards of Campos and dismounted. He thought that if he could stand between the rope and its target, he might be able to break up this nonsense.

Sutton slapped again, Campos jumped, and Thode threw his loop on the ground just behind Tony's boot heels. Sutton pulled his rope back and rebuilt his loop while Thode did the same. As Sutton came whipping down with his rope one more time, Clay moved forward. Campos jumped, Thode threw for the hocks, and Clay grabbed for the rope. He caught it and yanked, spooking the palomino. The horse cut away to the left and crow-hopped while Thode, his gloved hand still on the rope, was caught off-balance. A better roper than a rider, he went off the right side of the saddle. His boot hung in the stirrup, and as the horse bolted away it dragged the fallen rider. His head bounced, and the clean, high-crowned white hat rolled away.

Clay dashed for the horse, which by now had run up against the milling sheep and was stutter-stepping left and right. Clay laid a hand on the bridle in back of the bit and brought the horse to a standstill. Gathering the reins, he moved back to the right stirrup and freed Thode's foot. Then he stood back, wrinkling his nose at the stirred-up dust and the thick oily smell of sheep.

Sutton had pushed his horse past Campos and was stepping down. 'You all right, Alex?' he asked.

Thode rolled over to show a scratched and dirty face. Blood was oozing from a scrape on the forehead, and his left cheekbone was already beginning to swell. Bits of dead grass and smudges of dirt hung in the blond hair that was usually combed and clean.

'Are you all right, Alex?' Sutton repeated.

Thode's face was in a grimace and his brown eyes were watery, but he said, 'Yeah. I'm all right.'

Sutton reached a gloved hand down to Thode and said, 'Let me help you up.'

'I'll get up by myself,' Thode snapped. Then he rolled over, pushed himself up on to all fours, and stood up. Thode was tough – there was no question about that. He was in his mid-twenties and rock hard. He took the glove off his right hand and wiped his blond mustache.

Clay had not gotten a close look at Sutton before, and now he got a quick but full look. The man was not as big as he looked on horseback, but he was still a good two inches taller than Thode. In his early thirties, he was putting on weight and fleshing out in the face. The man was clean-shaven, and the straight brown hair was cut neatly, but the fleshy face had a sallow texture and seemed to carry dead weight. The gray eyes moved from Thode to Clay and back to Thode.

'Are you sure you're all right?' Sutton asked.

'Yeah, I'm fine,' Thode answered, feeling his swollen cheek, 'but I'll be better when I take care of this son of a bitch.'

'Not today. . . .' Sutton's glance flickered to Clay.

Thode seemed to make a point of not answering. He looked around for his hat, walked over, and picked it up. As he brushed the brim with his loose riding glove he said, 'No, not today.'

Sutton looked back at Clay. 'You bought yourself a good bunch of trouble, cowboy.' Then, as if remembering Campos, he looked back at the sheepherder and said, 'And the same goes for your Mexican friend here.'

Thode put on his hat and walked back toward Clay, who handed him the reins of the palomino. 'Don't ever touch my horse again,' he said, 'or my rope.' Thode went under the horse's neck to the other side, swung into the saddle, and started coiling in his rope.

11

'You two are real brave,' Clay said.

Thode's cheek was turning purple, and he grimaced as he spoke. 'Be brave enough for you when I catch up with you again,' he said, looking down at Clay. 'I won't put up with much from some dollar-a-day cowpuncher.'

'Or any two-bit Mexican,' Sutton added before he poked his foot into the stirrup and heaved himself up into the saddle.

Clay looked at Campos, whose face beneath the hat was deadpan.

Thode flopped his coiled rope against his right leg. 'Let's go, Ted.'

'All right.' As the two riders moved out, Sutton called back, 'You be lookin' over your shoulder from now on. The both of you.'

Clay shook his head as Sutton and Thode rode off. He was sure Sutton still didn't know him. Then he turned and walked toward Campos, who was standing ten yards away. 'I'm sorry if I made things worse for you. But I didn't like what I saw. It just burned me up.'

'I don't think they were gonna do too much.'

'I couldn't just stand there and watch you take it.'

'We learn to take a lot.'

'You don't have to.' Clay was close enough to read the other man's face. Campos was easygoing, but he wasn't soft.

'I know I don't have to,' he answered, 'but we learn to. This isn't the first time. The pretty one, he tried to run me off before. I just try to ignore 'em.'

'I guess I've got a short fuse. I've been told that.'

'Oh, I got my limit, too. Then watch out.' Tony flashed a white smile and his dark eyes sparkled.

Clay laughed. Tony was about forty years old, starting to gray around the temples and in the mustache, but he was sturdy. Everyone knew he was a good hand with a pitch-fork, ax, or shovel – tools that kept muscles and callouses on a man.

'Name's Clay Westbrook.' Clay offered his hand and Campos shook it.

'Tony Campos.'

'Well,' Clay said, 'I wonder if we'll have any trouble from those two.'

'If we do, we do. I guess we're partners, eh? You stuck up for me, and I'll stick up for you.'

'I guess so,' Clay replied.

'I kinda wish you wouldn't've done it,' Tony said. Then the white smile flashed and the eyes sparkled. 'But he sure looked like hell, didn't he?'

CHAPTER 2

The run-in with Sutton and Thode took place on a Sunday. By the middle of the week the story had traveled into the town, around the saloons, and back out into the cow country. Every time it was repeated, the story gathered and lost a few details. It was like the Cheyenne-to-Deadwood stage when it got to Lusk: it was the same coach, but there was a different driver, different horses, and some different passengers.

On Thursday, a WD rider who dropped off a bag of mail recounted the story for the Cross Pole hands. Clay was surprised to learn that he 'and a handful of Mexicans had jumped Sutton and Thode in the river bottom.'

After supper, when the men were back at the bunkhouse, everyone started joshing Clay about running with the desperadoes and carrying a knife in his boot. Cowboys who worked for an outfit were generally loyal to the brand they rode for and loyal to one another, until there was good reason not to be, so after a while the boys invited Clay to tell his version. He told it, including the parting threats from Sutton and Thode.

'What did the Mexican say?' asked Jamie Bellefleur, a cowpuncher from the Wolf River country the other side of Pierre.

'Actually, I thought he'd be a little more grateful. He said I probably didn't need to get into it, but since I did, he'd stick up for me if I needed it. Oh, and he also invited me to drop by next Sunday and eat with them.'

'With the gang?' Jamie teased.

'I think he meant his wife and kids.'

'I suppose so.' Jamie smiled. He was what some would call a pretty boy – a full head of wavy blond hair shading to light brown, dark blue eyes, and a light complexion that showed the flush of good health. He had a scar over his left eyebrow, and the scar danced when he smiled.

'You're goin to Meskin town, then,' said Highpockets.

'Uh-huh. I don't see any harm in it.'

'Oh, no,' Highpockets answered back. 'I've never been down there myself, but you see lotsa places like that back home.'

'Them Mexicans stick together,' said Two-Dollar Bill in a deadpan voice. Then he wrinkled his left nostril and said, 'Blood's thicker'n water.' Bill was from Texas, and like a lot of the punchers who had come up from Texas, he had an ingrained dislike for Mexicans. Clay had noticed that attitude before. At the moment, though, Clay couldn't tell if Bill meant it was good or bad that the Mexicans kept to themselves.

Jamie spoke up. 'All the same, it was nice of him to invite you, after you stuck up for him.'

'Well,' said Two-Dollar Bill, 'I don't know if I'd've gotten into it. You might be in for more trouble, and I don't think a Mexican is worth it.'

'I guess it was worth it to me,' Clay said. 'I couldn't stand to see two of them teamin' up on him.'

'Oh, yeah,' Bill said, turning his mouth down and shrugging. He pulled a bag of cigarette makings from his shirt pocket and said, 'Your business if you want to.'

'I'll tell you,' Clay said, 'this was the first time I really came close to Sutton.'

'He could make trouble,' said Bill, shaking tobacco into the paper trough.

Highpockets, another hand from Texas, spoke up. 'There are worse men around.' He was a few years older than Bill, pushing forty, and the oldest of the Cross Pole riders. He often spoke with an air of authority, although he wasn't bossy and never started arguments. If he ever disagreed very strongly, it was with Two-Dollar Bill. Then it was funny to listen to, with Highpockets' squeak and Bill's drawl.

'I don't know him. You say he's bad,' Jamie said to Bill, then

14

turned to Highpockets, 'and you say he's not so bad. What's Clay up against?'

Highpockets took the toothpick out of his mouth and put his foot up on the cold cast-iron stove. 'I'll tell you, Sutton came up the hard way and fought for what he's got, and if he's gotta poosh, he'll poosh hard.'

'You know him, then,' said Jamie.

'Know him and knew his father.' Highpockets seemed to enjoy having the attention.

'From way back?' asked Jamie.

'No, not way back. Just since the war. I met 'em both in the early eighties. The father was quite a fella. He went by Cap, since he'd made captain in the war.'

'Southern?' Clay asked.

'Oh, yeah. Louisiana. He'd lived quite a life. Went into the fur business just when the beaver market was goin' bust. Got outa that and went into the ice business with some fellas he'd met back East when he was sellin' furs. He was in that business for a while, then he mighta done somethin' else, I don't remember. Then come the war, and he went through that and come out sorta broken and bitter.'

'What about the son?' said Jamie.

Highpockets looked at the ceiling, then nodded. 'He'd a been born just before the war. He was in his early twenties when I met him, and that was ten years ago.'

'What did they do after the war?' Clay asked. He knew to phrase the question that way because the war was so much a part of the Southern mind, especially those who were Highpockets' age or older.

'Cap went to huntin' buffalo, and the boy went with him. He grew up in the huntin' camps, around all them rough men and hard drinkin'. Sort of a rag-tail kid, I think, but he come into his own. Then the old man died, not too long after I met 'em, and the buffalo was just about all killed off by then. But Ted wasn't like the general run of them fellas, and he didn't drink up every nickel he made. He bought an outfit and hired a couple of men and made a pretty good little pile of money in a couple of years, roundin' up buffalo bones.'

'That's a stinkin' job,' said Two-Dollar Bill. He squinted as he drew on his cigarette.

'It sure is, but he made a shit-pot full of money at it, and then he took up some land in Kansas. A little over a year ago, he come to Wyoming with a pretty good stake and started takin' up land here.'

'His land and cattle company seems to be more land than cattle,' Bill drawled.

'You could say that,' Highpockets squeaked back. 'He's a businessman, that's what. He don't truck so much in flies and cow shit like the rest of us do.'

Bill wasn't done. 'They say he has his cowboys file homesteading claims up and down all the streams, with the understandin' that it'll all go into his hands. Then he'll try to pinch out the little men.'

'Lots of big outfits do that. Whoever controls the water controls the land. It's not all wide open like it used to be.'

'I don't like 'im,' Bill drawled back. 'Not him or his fancy-ass little buddy.'

'Thode don't go a long way with very many people,' Highpockets said. 'Least of all, cowpunchers.'

'He's not gonna git much cow shit on him,' Bill said.

'No, I don't reckon he will.' Highpockets picked at his teeth and rubbed the stubble on his chin.

'It's because his old man has money, that's why he's prancin' around out here.' Bill tossed his cigarette stub out the open doorway.

'Probably so,' Highpockets answered. 'Them big-city fellas is good investors.'

'Uh-huh.' Bill took out his jackknife, which he kept razor sharp, and began cleaning his fingernails. He was called Two-Dollar Bill because he always kept two silver dollars in reserve so he would never be broke, but of course when he got down to those two dollars he was as good as broke. At those times he would say he was 'a little close' and ask to borrow from Highpockets, who kept a hoard of money. Highpockets never seemed to mind, since it gave him a kind of superiority in financial matters, and of course Bill always paid him back on payday.

'You wait and see,' Highpockets answered. 'When Sutton floats the deal on his ditch project, there'll be Eastern capital jinglin' like a Mexican's spurs.'

Jamie said, 'You seem to know a lot about this Sutton.'

Highpockets stood up and walked to the door to spit. 'Not so much. Nothin' you couldn't hear in any one of them honkatonks.'

Clay took a warning from that last remark.

As Highpockets stood lean-hipped and bony-shouldered with his back to the other men, it seemed as if he realized he had talked on long enough.

'Well,' said Two-Dollar Bill, 'I say he's a land grabber.'

Highpockets turned and walked slowly, as always, back to his chair. 'Might be.'

Clay looked at Highpockets, who generally had a lower-class look to him. His long, dark hair, not very thick, was combed behind his ears. He had dark, close-set eyes and a rough complexion. A person might have called him hatchet-faced except that his nose, in addition to being hooked, was broad and fleshy. The stubble on his chin and lean jaws looked dirty, as it usually did – he shaved about once a week. He was the kind of man who didn't drink and didn't spend money and who generally lived pretty tight and dry. He really wasn't Sutton's kind of man, but he took up for Sutton, and the way he did it gave Clay the impression that Highpockets would like to be affiliated with the big man. Highpockets would take some watching.

Jamie Bellefleur – or Jamie Belle, as he was often called – broke the silence. 'How many sheep did that Mexican have?'

'Probably about twenty. Why?'

'I was wonderin' if he'd have a job for you when Sutton buys the Cross Pole.'

Clay laughed. Jamie was all right. He was as good a friend as Clay had made in this country. Clay said, 'I'm glad you're lookin' out for me.' Clay had already decided to say nothing about Sutton's offer, so he left it at that.

Two-Dollar Bill spoke up. 'That'd be just about it, workin' fer a Mexican.'

Clay's temper flared up. 'I don't know what the difference would be,' he said. 'Work's work.'

17

'Mexicans is made to work for wages, not the other way around. I wouldn't work for one.'

Highpockets piped up. 'Them Meskins are all right. Good workers, some of 'em. Lot of 'em have no ambition, but some of 'em make good hands. You take that one that works for what's-his-name Randolph, right out of town there. He's a Meskin, and he's a good 'un.'

Clay burned quick again. 'What's his name?'

'Seems to me it's Hosay or one of them. I don't know for sure. Everyone just calls him Randolph's Meskin.'

'I'll give you one thing,' offered Two-Dollar Bill.

'What's that?' asked Clay.

'Them sinyoritas are all right. I been with a few of them.'

'Uh-huh.' Clay was not fond of Bill's attitude, but he found it more tolerable than Highpockets'.

'And I've even heard Sutton say he'd like to lay on one or two of them down in Mexican town,' Bill added.

'I thought you didn't like him,' Jamie said.

'I don't. But that don't mean he don't know nothin'.' Clay didn't even know a Mexican girl, but he felt himself despising Sutton all over again.

Two-Dollar Bill must have sensed that he had said something that rubbed Clay the wrong way, and he evidently tried to smooth things at Sutton's expense. 'Course, if I was him, I'd stick to chasin' blonde widders.'

Clay knew this was a reference to Louise Courtland, who held together a good-sized outfit down south of the Silver Plains spread. Her husband had been killed by lightning a few years back, and they did not have any children. It was generally understood that she was past childbearing age by now, but not by much. She was known as an attractive woman and very pleasant. That, along with her having a little money in the sack, gave her some prestige in a country short on women. In the cowboy code, men did not make or even tolerate ungallant remarks about nice women – 'widder' was a term that carried respect. Therefore, Clay perked up because it might tell him more about Sutton.

'You'd think so,' said Jamie Belle, in a tone that seemed to Clay to be deliberately innocent. Jamie knew how to keep Bill or

Highpockets talking.

Highpockets cut in. 'Man's business,' he said.

'Huh?' said Bill.

'I said it's a man's business.'

'Probably good business,' Bill answered. Then he raised his right boot and jingled his spur, which he was still wearing.

'What a man does with women is for him to talk about,' declared Highpockets. 'And besides, a woman should be good for something.'

No one spoke. Clay felt uneasy. Of course, a man's dealings with women were his own business, he thought, but Highpockets' comment wasn't made because of gallantry. He obviously didn't like Bill running on about Sutton.

Clay knew, as the others did, that Highpockets didn't seem to find any fun in woman talk. That part didn't bother Clay. He had known quite a few men who had no interest in women. They took to this kind of work, isolated from the lace and petticoats. When Clay heard remarks like that, he remembered what a Canadian cowboy named Artois had told him about men who didn't care about women. 'Don't bother about them. That's just one less to worry about.' At least with women, Clay thought, as he looked at Highpockets. Then Clay thought, *he'd probably cut my saddle cinch just to get on Sutton's good side.*

CHAPTER 3

Emerson Peck, the foreman of the Cross Pole, was somewhere into his fifties, older than any of the men who worked under him, and he didn't hide his age. He had a rounded, florid face, a gray drooping mustache, short gray hair on the temples, and a shiny bald head when he took off his round-brimmed Stetson. His wife was a plump Swedish woman who spoke fair English and smiled a lot. She kept her yellow hair in braids tied up around her head, and she seemed to be always wearing a broad white apron. The joke was that she must be a great cook, because of the way her husband's belly hung over his belt. He was a little above average height, and the extra weight seemed to cause him to lean forward.

Peck and his wife lived in the foreman's cabin. What kids they had were grown and gone, and Peck was said to be putting away his money ('rat-holing' it, as Highpockets put it) for whatever part of life's journey came after the Cross Pole Ranch. Peck had bossed on some big outfits in Nebraska and out that way, and the common view in the bunkhouse was that he was stopping over at the Cross Pole on his way to something bigger if he could find it. It was evident he liked being boss. He didn't like his authority being questioned, and as far as anyone knew, he never questioned the authority of the owners. They lived in St Louis, which seemed to suit him fine.

One way he had of being boss was to give orders on short notice. It seemed to Clay that Peck would rarely tell someone of a job a day ahead of time if he could save it until breakfast. Peck was usually up early, took in a full feed at his wife's table, and still had time to catch the cowboys while they were drinking coffee. On Friday morning, before Clay had finished his biscuits and gravy, Peck was standing over him. Clay was ordered to go to the Green Rock ranch, twelve miles to the north, to bring back a four-horse team and wagon that Peck had loaned out on an exchange of favors.

Clay nodded, and Peck moved on to the other men. Clay half-heard their talk as he cleaned his plate. Then he motioned to Highpockets, who poured him his second cup of coffee. This wasn't roundup, he thought, when a man had to gulp and run. Spring gather was coming up, and although Peck hadn't said so, that was why Clay was fetching the wagon and horses. Roundup would be here soon enough, and he thought he might as well enjoy a cup of coffee while he could.

Later, as he was heading for Green Rock, Clay thought about what a pretty morning it was to be riding north, or to be riding anywhere, for that matter. The sun came up in a glow of pink and yellow, then rose quickly. The air warmed up, the shadows crawled back, and the country spread out wide all around him. In the full sunlight the prairie flowers stood out, most notably the sand lily, with its long white spindly petals, and the phlox, with its star pattern of five rounded petals. Clay thought, if he had a girl, now would be the time to think of her.

There was no breeze yet, just the clear morning air. Clay was riding a gray ranch horse, a fast and smooth walker he'd picked out for today's job. The steady clip-clop of the hoofs was a pleasant sound, interrupted only by the tink-a-link of a meadowlark now and then.

Off to the left a hundred yards, seemingly out of nowhere, a band of a half dozen antelope materialized. They trotted away to the northwest, suddenly cut to the left and, flashing their white rumps in the morning sun, took off due west, stirring up a low cloud of dust in their wake. A half mile farther on, in the shadows of a draw to the east, he saw three deer, mule-eared and dusky, feeding along.

The sun climbed higher and warmed Clay's back. In a dry wash he stopped his horse and dismounted, watered a wild rose bush that was leafing out, and tied his wool jacket on to the back of his saddle with his slicker. He mounted up and rode on. He would get a drink of water at the Green Rock.

About four miles out from the ranch, as he guessed it, he saw a dark form ahead of him and off the trail to the left a few yards. It was probably a dead cow, one that hadn't made it through the winter. As the horse brought him closer, Clay saw that it was indeed a dead cow, lying on its right side with its head pointed north toward the ranch. The carcass had been pretty well picked over and cleaned out, but a good piece of the hide, dry now, still stretched over it. Out of habit, Clay rode toward it to see if there was a brand to read, but all he got for his effort was a good whiff of dead cow.

The smell of the dead animal and the sight of the white ribs and leg bones reminded Clay of the conversation the night before. He wrinkled his nose. This used to be Sutton's line of work. A lot of what he picked up would have been bleached bones and skulls from years past, but it wasn't all clean as ivory. Bones paid by the pound, all the better when they were wet with rain or snowmelt. A skeleton from winterkill, not yet dried out, added handsomely to the pile.

Clay tried to picture Sutton, a rag-tail kid as Highpockets had called him, growing up with the lice and the rank greasy smells of the buffalo hunters' camps. Clay had met a few old-time buffalo hunters and had heard about others, and they were an unwashed bunch. So were the bone hunters.

Sutton had earned his first pile of money the hard way, Clay thought. He had to give him that. Clay imagined Sutton in the ugly labor of those years, looking forward to the time when he might have money, land, and men under him. And the likes of Alex Thode.

Well, he thought, Sutton was a big man now. He obviously thought he could hire men away from other outfits, men he didn't even know. When Clay first heard the offer he took it as a compliment, thinking his reputation as a good cowhand had gotten around. From the way the offer was made, though, he thought he had better not make too quick a decision. Now that he had had the run-in with Sutton, he assumed Sutton would connect the name and the person, and the offer, which Clay had not really considered very much anyway, would be void by now. It was just as well. He had taken a dislike to Sutton, even more so after the bunkhouse talk. It would be better to steer clear of him.

Clay got a long drink of water at the Green Rock headquarters and washed his face as well, trying to clear out the smell of the dead cow. Then he rode out with another hand to bring in the horses. He brushed them down and checked their feet, then hitched them to the wagon. After that he tied the gray horse to the tail end of the wagon, pulled off the saddle and blanket, and laid them in the wagon box. He ate a quick and early lunch in the cook-house and was on his way back to the Cross Pole.

On his return he stayed clear of the dead cow, but a trace of it came drifting his way. It made him think of Sutton again – Sutton, the scavenger turned proud and greedy land grabber. Sutton, who wanted to cut a big ditch and sell water to the punkin rollers. Sutton, who was after the blonde widow but wanted to lay on a Mexican girl.

Clay felt a knot in his stomach, and his teeth were clenched. He wanted to hit Sutton. He wanted to pull him off that long-legged horse and pound him into the ground. If Sutton came at him on foot Clay would go for the knees. That was the way with a big, top-heavy man. Knock his knees out from under him, maybe drop your own weight, with one knee, into his ribs or his arm socket. Or knock the wind out of him, get him flat on his back, and pound at his face. Hit him. Pound him. If it was Lance Murdock, Clay would let him get up on all fours and kick him in the face.

Clay exhaled heavily and widened his eyes. His heartbeat had picked up and his mouth was dry. *Lance Murdock.* He shook his head. He had tried not to think of him because of the way it tied his guts up. Murdock was the only man he had ever really hated. Thinking about Sutton had reopened a wound, calling up raw pain as he thought about Murdock and Rosalind. They were from a different time and place, almost from a different life, but the memory could burn into him like a red-hot iron as he sat on the wagon seat heading south on a sunny spring day.

Clay had met Lance Murdock in the John Day country of eastern Oregon, where Clay grew up. They worked together on the same ranch the year Clay turned twenty. The next spring, after the bad winter of 1886–87, Clay and Lance signed on to drive a herd of Durham cattle to the Yellowstone country. It promised to be an adventure for the two young men, and they expected to be back in the fall. Clay said goodbye to Rosalind with long and lingering kisses, and asked her to wait for him. She said she would.

One night after they had crossed into Idaho, the trail boss found a pasture to put the herd into for the night, and he let the cowboys have a night in town. Clay and Lance had a few drinks, and Clay got to talking about how much he missed Rosalind. Lance, who was a few years older than Clay but didn't hold his liquor any better, let it out that he was in love with her, too. But he said he wasn't going to do anything about it – that is, he wasn't going to set his cap for her. Maybe this trip would help him get over her, and if not, he would just move on. He blubbered on that way, and like a good drunk he pledged eternal friendship to Clay. As Clay remembered it, it all seemed both ordinary and unreal – Murdock's flushed face, his arm across Clay's shoulder, his repeated promises, his self-pity and self-deprecation.

It made Clay sick to remember, but he couldn't forget the repeated phrases. 'It's rotten of me to feel the way I do, but I can't

help myself,' and 'You're the best friend I've ever had,' and 'I
don't care if it kills me, but I'm not going to do anything about
it. I couldn't let myself make a play for her.'

In the morning, Clay rolled out later than usual, his head thick
from the night before.

Lance Murdock was gone, having gotten up before dawn and
settled with the boss for a saddle horse and half his wages. That
wasn't all that was gone. So was Clay's photograph of Rosalind, in
its oval frame of gold.

Even without the portrait, Clay still had a perfect picture of
her – hair the color of wheat straw, eyes as blue as bachelor
buttons. He remembered how warm she was when he held her
close, warm and moist when he kissed her. Rosalind had smiled
whenever she saw him, talked about the future with him, had
tears in her eyes when he left. Rosalind Lea. He had asked her to
wait, and she had said that she would. They had agreed to write
to each other at several stops along the trail drive.

By the time he got to Butte, Montana, he had written a letter
to her, but he didn't mail it because he got hers first. It had been
posted as they had agreed. His hands were shaking as he cut open
the envelope and took out the letter.

She was sorry, she said, to hear what he had done. She
understood why he might get drunk, she might even have
forgiven him for bedding with an Indian woman, but she
couldn't forgive him for tossing her photograph on the ground
and telling Lance to take it. Lance was ashamed of him, and she
was, too. She wasn't going to wait anymore. By the time he
received her letter, she said, she would have married Lance
Murdock and moved to the Willamette Valley.

Clay was stunned. When Murdock first left, Clay thought that
maybe it had been shame – too embarrassed to look Clay in the
eye after confessing has feelings for Rosalind. Then, the more he
thought about it, especially about the missing photograph, the
more he thought Murdock might make a play for Rosalind after
all. But never did he dream that Lance would twist things the way
he did.

It stood to reason, though. The man was a traitor – a liar and
a thief. Once he had lied to Clay and stolen from him, it was

natural that he should follow through and lie to Rosalind. But it was crazy. How would he expect to get away with it? If Clay came to their doorstep, would he still lie? Did he expect Clay not to come after them? Did he even think that far ahead, or was he so sick that he just lived from one lie to the next for as long as he could get away with it?

To make sense of it, Clay tried to determine the point at which Lance first lied to him. Maybe it was when they signed on for the cattle drive. Maybe it was before that. It could have been as late as the night they got drunk, but even at that point, Lance might have thought he was telling the truth.

Maybe he always thought he was telling the truth. Clay had heard of people like that but had never met one. They would lie even if the truth were better, and they had no shame if they were caught in a lie. They might be brazen enough to deny it was a lie, or they might move to another one.

Finally he gave up trying to understand it. It didn't matter why the man had done him that way. He had done it, and when Clay got back to Oregon he would hunt him down and make him pay.

The desire for revenge kept Clay going to the end of the drive. He lived on the idea, feeding on it as it fed on him. When they delivered the herd at Bozeman, he was all set to buy the fastest horse he could find and head back to Oregon.

By then he had gotten a letter from home that confirmed what he feared. Rosalind was married and gone. The letter put him on the edge even more, all set to go back and settle a score. But then something happened. He found himself looking at a new pistol, thinking he would buy it along with a camp outfit for the trip back. The six-shooter was clean and shiny and smelled like gun oil. The cylinder clicked in a way that pleased him. He was about to buy the gun when he set it down on the counter and walked outside to sit on the board sidewalk.

It was as if he had just come out of a daze. He didn't need another gun; he had one. And he wouldn't do any good by going back and killing Lance Murdock. It wouldn't get Rosalind back. It would just land him in prison. He realized there was really nothing he could do about the betrayal but hold a grudge. That was the only way he could go on living his own life.

That's how he saw it that day as he sat on the sidewalk with his boot heels in the gutter. There was a man he would always hate, but there were a thousand miles and two mountain ranges between them, and he might just keep it that way.

For a while he knocked around on his own – just himself, a saddle horse, and a packhorse. He drifted up toward Great Falls and the upper Missouri country, and he got it into his head that maybe he should just go ahead and lay up with an Indian. He did that in Great Falls, but it didn't seem to make a bit of difference. After that he went back to the idea that there wasn't much he could do except try to live through it – and hold a grudge.

Over five years had passed, and Clay had found a part of the country here in Wyoming that seemed like it could be home. He never thought of Montana, beautiful country that it was, without a lurch in his stomach. When he thought of Oregon, as he did now, sitting on the wagon seat, he thought of the miles and the mountains, and he nodded.

Clay looked off to the west and saw only rippling plains, fading to a shadowy purple in the distance. It was a good country, he thought, and life had been getting good again until this trouble with Sutton had come up. Even though he tried not to, few days went by without his thinking of Lance Murdock and hating him. But lately he had felt a little zest for life, and he could look to the future with optimism. But now there was this thing with Sutton, like a dark cloud on the prairie, and here he was thinking about Murdock.

When he looked into his own feelings, something kicked when he brought up an image of Sutton. It was strong, but it wasn't hatred. There had been a stretch of time when he would have killed Murdock if he had met him in a coulee up in the Missouri breaks. He even looked for him, although he knew full well the man was a thousand miles away. He didn't feel that way toward Sutton, and yet he couldn't say that his feelings for Sutton and for Murdock were completely separate.

Maybe it had something to do with Louise Courtland. Clay had never actually seen her. He had heard of her, and he had an image of her. In his mind's eye she was a middle-aged version of Rosalind.

26

CHAPTER 4

During round-up time there was no such thing as Sunday: every day was a work day until the job was done. It wasn't roundup time yet, though. That was still over a week away, so when Sunday came around, it was a day off for the Cross Pole boys. Sometimes when they had a Sunday off they would ride into town on Saturday night, let the animal loose a little bit, and then either sleep over in town or come trailing back in the wee hours before dawn. On this Saturday, however, since Two-Dollar Bill was 'a little close' on his money and Clay had a social engagement for Sunday, the boys decided to wait until midmorning on Sunday to ride in. Highpockets wasn't going anyway, and Jamie wasn't one to burn down the honky-tonks, so nobody was put out.

They spent Saturday night in the bunkhouse. Highpockets didn't gamble, so until Peck put on a couple of more men for the summer work there wouldn't be any poker games. Highpockets didn't consider cribbage to be gambling, though; he considered it a game of skill. He had a cribbage board made out of an elk antler, a set that used to belong to Two-Dollar Bill, and the two of them often passed the time at night playing cribbage. They played for half a penny a point, 'to make it interesting,' as they said, and the games were usually close enough that not much money changed hands when they settled up on paydays. So on Saturday night, Bill and Highpockets played cribbage, Jamie read a couple of newspapers that had come with Thursday's mail, and Clay mended a shirt.

On Sunday morning, after the three men had cleaned up and shaved, they got into their town clothes and saddled their horses. Clay saddled his private horse, the sorrel he called Rusty. On Cross Pole time he rode ranch horses, but on a day like today he would take out his own horse to keep him in shape. Two-Dollar Bill took his own horse, a dark brown gelding that was almost black, while Jamie had his buckskin. As they were coming out of the barn, Clay noticed that Bill was wearing his six-gun.

'Goin' armed, Bill?'

Bill winked. 'This is the time of year the snakes come out. Was I you, I'd at least put one in the saddle-bag.'

Clay nodded and followed the advice, going back into the bunkhouse and putting on his .45 for the ride into town. As they were mounting up, he noticed that Jamie was wearing his pistol, as well.

They rode three abreast, Bill in the middle. Bill was nearly ten years older than Clay and made it known that he had been on his own since he was fourteen. He took the role of the older man, wise to the world, when he was around Clay and Jamie. If someone knew when to pack a pistol, he did. Clay looked at him as they rode. Bill had evidently been around, even if he was sometimes vague about where. He gave his name as Bill Fulton and said he was from Texas. Once, when one of the summer hands asked him what part of Texas, he drawled, 'Whah, just about all over.' He was pure Texas cowboy, as Clay saw him. Medium height and lean, he was a natural in the saddle. He was proud to say he wore out his boots on top of the toes before the soles gave out, and he hated working with a shovel. He could rope with the best of them, tied hard and fast, Texas style. Even if he had some attitudes that rubbed on Clay, he was a top hand and would stick by the fellows he rode with.

Clay looked at Jamie, in his clean white shirt and red bandana. Jamie was a good hand, too – good bronc rider and a good man with a rope. He was a crack shot with a rifle, also, and he kept in practice by shooting prairie dogs on his time off. Jamie was easygoing and knew how to stay out of trouble, but Clay knew he could count on his friend if anything got started.

Two-Dollar Bill began to sing. He seemed to be in a good mood, maybe because he was going to town where he could wet his whistle. He had a good singing voice, and he carried a tune better than a lot of cowboys.

Well, I went down south for to see my gal,
   Sing polly-wolly-doodle all day,
My Sal she am a spunky gal,
   Sing polly-wolly-doodle all day.

My Sal she am a maiden fair,
   Sing polly-wolly-doodle all day,
With laughing eyes and golden hair,
   Sing polly-wolly-doodle all day.

Jamie Belle interrupted. 'Isn't it "curly" hair? That's how I heard it.'

'I'll tell ya,' answered Bill. 'There's not a lot of that song I do know.'

'You never hear a song sung the same way twice, anyway,' said Clay.

'Hell, no,' Bill agreed. 'Next fella comes up the trail'll give 'er raven hair.'

'Let's give her golden hair,' said Jamie, 'and we'll all sing it.'

'Fine by me,' Bill said. 'Lemme sing out the last verse that I do know, and then we'll run through the whole thing a few times.'

'Sing 'er,' said Jamie.

Bill took it up. 'Here goes:

Fare thee well, fare thee well,
Fare thee well, my fairy fay,
For I'm goin' to Loosiana for to see my Susyanna
Singin' polly-wolly-doodle all day.'

So they sang, three cowboys light of heart on a sunny spring day. They sang the polly-wolly-doodle song a dozen times before they got tired of it, and then they moved on to others, with jokes about Sal and Lulu in between. The miles flowed beneath them, and the sun was just straight up when they came to the edge of town.

They took the wide road in from the west. At the center of town the other two riders turned left to find their billiard parlor, and Clay turned right. This road led south over the river, and on the other side of the plank bridge was Mexican town.

Clay had been past this little bunch of houses before, but he hadn't been down any of the streets or even paid much attention from the outside. He did know that the Mexican folks lived there by sort of a mutual agreement with the rest of the town. They kept to themselves and did things their way, and they were generally left alone. Now, as Clay headed toward the little community, he felt a nervousness in his stomach.

Rusty's hoofs thumped across the plank bridge, and it sounded loud to Clay, loud enough to announce his arrival. He looked ahead, but no one was out looking for him. It occurred to him that Campos's people were used to the sounds of horses and wagons crossing the bridge.

The row of houses along the road was facing east, away from the road and into the little town. What a traveler saw from the road was a backyard view of chicken houses, live-stock pens, woodpiles, and clotheslines. As Clay turned off the road and on to the lane that curved into the village, he saw that there were four rows of houses, parallel. There was a wide dirt street between the first and second rows that faced each other, a narrower street or alley between the backs of the second and third, and a wide street again between the last two rows. A quick glance told him there were a couple of dozen buildings. Some had clapboard, some were made of lumber and tarpaper, and some were stuccoed. From the little he knew of Mexican towns, he imagined some of the buildings might be stores or small businesses where people took in washing, did sewing, or sold items of food like tortillas or tamales. At the far end, the south end, was a larger white building that he knew served as a community hall where the people had their own church services, festivals, and dances. Clay knew that a priest came here every other Sunday, and he wondered if today was one of those days.

Following the lane into the first street, Clay saw a woman a couple of houses ahead on the right, sweeping in front of her house. As he rode closer he saw that it was an area about ten feet square, paved with flat rocks set in hard-packed dirt. It looked like a good place to sit in the shade on a sunny afternoon. The middle of the street was lower than either side, so he edged up to ask directions from the lady. She was middle-aged, with shoulder-length hair, not slender and not heavy. She wore a dark blue dress and black shoes.

'Tony Campos?' he called out.

She pointed up and over, to signify that Campos lived down the next street.

Clay smiled and nodded, and the woman smiled up at him, brushing her hair back. As Clay touched his spurs to Rusty, he noticed the woman looking at his gun. He winced. She could be thinking he came to start trouble. At the end of the street he dismounted, stowed his gunbelt in the saddle-bag, and led the horse to the next street. This was better, he thought, not to be looking down at people.

Down the second main street on his left he saw another lady, a little heavier than the first, also sweeping. As he came closer he saw that it was just an apron of hard-packed dirt, but she had it swept clean of twigs and chicken feathers. Now he noticed chickens down the street, white chickens and brown ones, poking in and out of the shadows. A dog stood up in the doorway behind the woman and barked. The woman held the broom in her left hand, and with her right hand she waved downward at the dog to shut him up.

'Tony Campos?' Clay asked.

'*Un momento*,' she said, and stepped through the open doorway and called what seemed like a person's name. Then she said something in a long smooth sentence, and a boy about ten years old came out, smiling and squinting.

He had straight black hair cut above the ears, a plain cotton shirt, and similar trousers. He was barefoot, and he shaded his eyes with his right hand as he spoke to Clay. 'Come with me. I show you where is the Campos house.'

Clay said thanks, then nodded to the senora, who smiled back at him from the doorway.

The boy led Clay down the street and across the way to a stuccoed house. He rapped at the open doorway and said something in Spanish. Then he returned to Clay, who was tying his horse to the rear wheel of a wagon that didn't look like it was going anywhere.

'That's a pretty horse,' the boy said.

'Thanks. I call him Rusty.'

The boy nodded without showing that he understood. Then he said goodbye and walked back toward his house.

Tony came to the doorway and spoke out. 'Hello, partner. How are you? Come in.' He motioned with his arm as he stood there, hatless and in stockinged feet.

'I'm fine, Tony. How are you?' Clay shook his hand and walked into the front room of the house.

The room seemed dark at first in contrast to the brightness outside, but Clay adjusted. He looked into a dark corner for a moment and then back at the center of the room. Light was coming in through a window and through the open doorway, and he could see pretty well. In the center of the room was a wooden table surrounded by half a dozen chairs. In back of the living room was an open archway that led to the kitchen, and across the table from where he stood was a door that led to another part of the house, presumably sleeping quarters.

'Sit down,' Tony said. 'We're gonna eat in a little while.'

Clay sat down, looking at Tony as he did so. The man had a full head of wavy, black hair, combed back and showing a few strands of gray. When he smiled, as before, his white teeth flashed and his dark eyes sparkled.

A woman about Tony's age, presumably his wife, appeared at the archway and said something.

Tony looked at her and then back at Clay. 'Would you like something? Coffee? Beer?'

'A beer sounds as good as anything right now.'

'Sure.' Tony spoke back at the woman, who called into the back part of the house that led from the kitchen. In a couple of minutes a boy a little older than the boy in the street came out of the kitchen, swinging a half-gallon cream can by the handle. He stopped at Tony's chair, got a silver dollar and a hair rumpling, and skipped out. 'My son,' Tony said.

'How many do you have?'

Tony took a deep breath. 'Six. You know, still living. The two girls are married. They got their own houses over there in New Mexico. They're the oldest. Then I got these four boys. Good boys.'

Clay nodded.

'You got kids?'

'No, I've never been married.'

'You got plenty of time.'

'Oh, yeah.'

'They wanna get married so young. Both my girls at sixteen.'

'Uh-huh.'

'I hope my boys wait. It's too hard.'

'Uh-huh.'

Tony took out a sack of Bull Durham and offered it to Clay, who declined. Tony rolled a smoke, popped a match, and lit it.

The boy came back into the house and carried the cream can to the kitchen. Then he brought the change to his father.

'This is my son, Marcos.'

'My name's Clay Westbrook.' Clay stood halfway up, leaned across the table, and shook hands with the lad.

The boy said something in Spanish as if excusing himself, and he left the room as his mother came in carrying two glasses of beer. She was a slender woman, not very tall, with dark brown hair down past her shoulders.

'This is my wife, Margarita. That means, Daisy, the flower.'

'You can call me Daisy,' she said, smiling, 'or Margarita.'

'All right. I'm Clay,' he said, rising and holding out his hand. Then for the first time he remembered to take off his hat.

'Please to meet you,' she said, with a hard s. She had dark brown eyes with crow's feet at the corners, which made her look tired until she smiled. 'I go to cook,' she said, and went back to the kitchen.

The men turned to their beer, lifted the glasses, and clicked them.

'*Salud*,' said Campos.

'Salooth.'

After a little while, Tony spoke. 'You haven't had no more trouble with the bigshots, have you?'

'No, not yet.'

Campos broadened his nostrils and relaxed them. 'I don't know them, really. I barely know their names now.'

'I don't either, to speak of, but I gather that Sutton wants to own the whole country and run it his way.'

Tony nodded. 'Oh, yeah. He's that way. You can tell it.'

'I don't like him or the way he acts.'

Tony laughed. '*Tranquilo, muchacho*. You gotta take it easy.'

'I get mad.'

'I get mad, too, but I learned to take it.'

'I know. You said that the other day. But I'm not goin' to let someone push me around.'

'That's a difference,' Campos said. 'You got a different life.'

'What do you mean?'

Tony got up and walked to the open door, where he pinched out his cigarette and tossed the butt outside. After he sat back down, he said, 'You know, the *mexicano* sees the world different. If something's gonna happen, or not happen, you can't do much to change it. They teach us that in the church, we see it in the government and the people who have everything. We been takin' it for a long time – the church, the rich people, the weather, death – you learn to take it. My wife and me, we lost two little babies. We couldn't do nothin' about that.'

'Uh-huh.'

'It's like the weather. You get a bad snow and it kills half your cows. What do you do?'

'Start over, I guess.'

'You take it.'

'Sure. You can't do anything about it.'

'Over there in Mexico, if a man treats me like that, I kill him and then I have to fight his brothers, and they have to fight my brothers. But if he's rich, or with the *federales*, I just take it. Then it's like the weather.'

'That's how you see Sutton and Thode, then?'

'I can't fight all the white people, not in their country, so I ain't gonna start with the bigshots. But if he does something to me,' and he pointed with his four fingers at the center of his chest, 'or my family,' and he waved his left hand toward the kitchen, 'and I catch him alone, ay, *chihuahua*, I kill him like a pig.' He laughed, a good short deep laugh. 'But some bigshots that don't like my sheep? I can take a little of that.' And he brushed away Sutton and Thode with the back of his hand.

'How about what he said about—' Clay paused. 'Mexicans?'

Tony shook his head. 'That's too stupid to kill someone. He don't even know me.'

'Well, it burned the hell out of me.'

'Me too, but I can take that much.' Tony shrugged and took out the makings for another cigarette.

While they had been talking, Clay had become aware of two female voices in the kitchen. Apparently there were two women fixing dinner. The good smells of a Mexican kitchen were starting to drift out, along with the sound of food frying.

Margarita came from the kitchen and took their empty glasses. She was back almost immediately with the two glasses brimming as before.

Clay smiled and thanked her. The beer was still cool and tasted good, and he was getting interested in what the dinner would be like.

When they finished the second beer, Tony invited Clay to go out and see the garden. They went out the front door so Clay could check on his horse, which was doing fine.

In back of the house, looking out into open prairie, was Campos's garden. It was probably a quarter of an acre, neatly furrowed and recently planted. Tony showed Clay the tomatoes, the various kinds of peppers, the onions and garlic, the carrots, potatoes, melons, and corn – all seedlings and just pushing out into plants.

'How do you water all this?' Clay asked.

Tony pointed to a hand pump by the back door. 'I get plenty of water this close to the river,' he said, 'and I got four boys.'

Clay nodded. Then he thought of something. 'Where are your sheep?'

Campos pointed north, in the direction of the river. 'I got them in a pen at the end. No one uses it, so I got my sheep there.'

'You haul water to them?'

'Usually me or my boys, we let 'em drink at the river. You wanna go see 'em?'

Remembering the smell of the sheep as it had hung in his nose the week before, he said, 'No hurry. I can see 'em another time. You keep goats too?'

'Right now I got no goats, but I usually got a couple. You want one?' Tony flashed his smile.

Clay smiled back. 'No, I don't need one. I just didn't remember seeing any last week.'

'I'll probably have some later.'

'Uh-huh.'

Back inside the house, Clay was glad to see Margarita setting a stack of tortillas, wrapped in a towel, on the table. 'Pretty soon,' she said, and went back into the kitchen.

Tony motioned for Clay to sit down, and he did. As he was pulling the chair under him, he looked up to see a young woman carrying two plates of food from the kitchen. A lamp had been lit and set on a sideboard, and as the woman moved into the lamplight, Clay caught his breath. She was beautiful.

She had thick, dark hair that cascaded below her shoulders. It was combed back from her smooth forehead, which glistened from the work in the kitchen. Her eyebrows were dark and her eyelashes were long, accentuating the large eyes that were dark as black coffee. She had smooth brown skin and red lips that drew the eye. She wore a tan dress with an apron over it, but there was no mistaking that she was shapely. She smiled as she set down the plates in front of Tony and Clay, and as she walked away through the lamplight, Clay could not keep his eyes from following her. He breathed again, and he could feel his heart beating.

Tony helped himself to a tortilla and motioned to his guest to do the same. Clay gave a questioning motion with his head, in the direction that the young woman had just gone.

'My niece.'

'Oh.' Clay was in a daze. He saw Tony begin to eat, tearing a piece off the flour tortilla and using it like a spoon with no handle. Clay did likewise, eating the piece of tortilla with the food it held. The plate had two large portions of food – refried beans, and cubed meat swimming in a sauce of tomatoes, peppers, and onions. Clay looked up as he chewed the food. He tasted beans. He remembered scooping them into the piece of tortilla. Time seemed to stand still. Then the girl came out with two more plates of food. He looked at her but she didn't look back. He took a deep breath and bent his head to eat as she walked back to the kitchen.

Clay kept his eyes on his plate for several minutes as he ate. During that time the four boys came to the table. He looked around at them and nodded. The two youngest, who were in the range of seven to nine years old, were sharing a chair. The other two boys were each taking up one chair, and there was one seat open. Both women were still in the kitchen.

Clay was cleaning his plate when the young woman took her place at the end of the table near the kitchen. Margarita stood at the threshold between the kitchen and the eating area. Clay half-rose from his chair and motioned to his place, to offer it to her.

She smiled and said, 'No, thank you. Later.' Then she gestured around the table, suggesting that she was there to serve more food as needed. She asked, 'More?' and when Clay answered, 'Yes, please,' she came around to his place and took his plate. When she brought it back she spoke to Tony and took his plate to the kitchen.

Tony made a small exclamation in Spanish and then said, 'Clay, this is my niece, Lupita. Lupita, this is my friend, Clay.'

Lupita nodded and smiled a closed-mouth smile.

Clay nodded and said, 'Pleased to meet you.' He wondered if she spoke English.

One by one the boys finished eating and left the table. Each one said the same short phrase, which sounded like the one the oldest boy had said earlier. When the last one left, Clay looked at Tony and asked, 'What are they saying?'

Lupita must have thought he was asking her. She looked up and said, '*Con permiso.* It means they're asking to be excused.'

Clay smiled and she smiled back. He noticed her lips weren't as red as they were earlier. She must have rubbed them clean before she sat down to eat.

Now Margarita sat down with a plate of food, a good healthy serving for herself. Clay noticed a resemblance between the two women, Lupita being a little taller and larger.

Clay finished his second plate, declined a third helping, and sat quietly for a few minutes. Then he put himself up to ask, 'Are you visiting here, miss?'

She looked at him rather seriously, it seemed, and said, 'No, I live here.'

'Oh. I hadn't seen you before.'

'I don't think you've visited here before, have you?'

'No, but I meant I hadn't seen you around town.'

'I don't go out very much. I just go to work and back. And I help my aunt. *Verdad, tía?*'

Margarita looked at Clay and smiled. 'Oh, yes. She help me all the time.'

Clay nodded and then asked Lupita, 'Where do you work?'

'At the bakery,' she said. She finished her plate and pushed it away.

'How do you like that?'

'It's hot and it's dry, but—'

'But what?'

'I put up with it.'

Clay wondered at her hesitation, and then it occurred to him that she must have overheard her uncle earlier when he said they learned to take it, and she must have paused to think of a different way to say it in English. Then he said, 'I don't get to town much. That's probably why I've never seen you.'

'Oh,' she said, 'do you work on a ranch?'

Clay was pretty sure she already knew the answer, what with the way he looked and the way he had talked with her uncle, but he answered her directly. 'Yes, I work on the Cross Pole, about seventeen miles out.'

'Oh.'

Then he thought, what the hell, she's got to know I'm the one who stuck up for her uncle. So he said, 'I'm the fella that was with your uncle down by the river last Sunday. I suppose he told you about it.'

Lupita glanced at her uncle, who was rolling a cigarette and pretending not to pay attention. Then she said, 'No, he didn't say anything.'

'Oh. Then I'm sorry I brought it up.'

'Don't worry. I mean, that's all right. I heard about it anyway. And I saw the poor boy you beat up. His face looks terrible.'

Clay's heart sank. He didn't want to make things worse, but he couldn't let it go at that. 'I didn't beat him up,' he said, 'but I guess I did cause him to fall off his horse and get dragged.'

She paused, looking at the table. Then she looked up. 'I shouldn't have said it that way,' she said. 'I wasn't there, and besides, it was between you men.' She looked at her uncle.

Tony shook out his match and blew smoke. 'He sure looks bad, all right. I seen him yesterday.' Then he turned to Lupita and said, 'Clay thinks he wants a goat.'

'Really?' she said, bringing her brows together.

'I think he's teasing,' Clay said, drawing his own eyebrows down and half-smiling.

'Well,' she said, 'if you want to find a goat, he can help you.'

She rose from her chair, picked up her plate, smiled at Clay, and said, '*Con permiso.*' Then she went into the kitchen.

When Tony finished his smoke he got up and tossed the pinched stub outside. Clay could hear the dishes rattling in the kitchen where the two women were. Tony came back and stood by the table, yawning and stretching.

'I gotta go over to the stockyards and make sure the cattle all got water.'

'You walk or ride?' Clay asked.

'I got a horse. I just gotta bring him in.'

'You have him staked out?'

'Yeah.'

'I'll go with you.'

'Sit here and take it easy.'

'All right. Then I'll ride with you as far as the stockyards.'

The women were still in the kitchen when Tony was ready to go. Clay got up from the chair where he had been half-dozing and went to the kitchen to pay his respects. He thanked Margarita for the fine meal, and he shook her hand. Then he touched Lupita's hand for the first time as he said goodbye to her.

'I hope you didn't get a bad first impression of me,' he said.

She looked at him as if it mattered. 'Oh, you mean about the fight? No, not really. And it's in the past anyway, isn't it?'

CHAPTER 5

As they were leaving the Campos household, Tony made a point of telling Clay that this would always be his house, that he was always welcome for any reason. Clay thanked him. Then they rode across the plank bridge and on to the stockyards. Tony invited Clay to come for dinner again the following Sunday. Then they shook hands, and Clay rode away. He had the feeling that he had been through a process and had followed form pretty well.

Still in the afterglow of having met Lupita, he felt the urge to take a look at his hundred and sixty acres. Jamie and Bill weren't waiting for him, and there was plenty of daylight left, so he headed for the river. He forded it near the scene of the previous week's scuffle, and soon he was up on higher ground, heading west on a sunny afternoon.

Once he was on the south side of the river, Clay had a general sense of being in Sutton's territory. The Silver Plains interests lay south and were spread out over quite a bit of that country. The remarks in the bunkhouse a few nights earlier suggested that some of the Silver Plains riders might even have taken up claims along Saddle Creek. He had paid to have the land surveyed and staked, and he had had his claim recorded in good black ink in the US Land Office, so he imagined any cowpunchers like himself would respect the claim and leave it alone.

Clay had seen nesters who had hooked up a prairie plow first thing and cut a furrow all the way around. Others, especially if they controlled good water, put up a barbed-wire fence and cut their parcel off from the rest of the range. Clay had ridden the open country for long enough already that he wanted to leave his part open until he had to do otherwise. He would have boundaries either way, and as long as he knew where they were, that was good enough.

Saddle Creek ran almost due north along the western edge of his claim, so he turned left at the creek and, from the higher ground, followed it upstream. The plains country was full of dips and rises. If a person looked down on it and across a distance it looked flat, and he could see another rider miles away. When he was down in the country, though, even the flattest country had surprises, such as the antelope he had bumped into on his ride north. If he was going to get back to the ranch at any decent hour, he was going to have to ride pretty directly. Still, he picked his trail so he could watch the country from the high points as he went. It was habit anyway, from looking for cattle, but today he also stopped for a moment here and there in the shadow of a cutbank or at the rim of a rise.

He picked places that gave him a good view of the land. In one such place, from behind a small knob covered with soapweed and prickly pear, he saw a rider headed north-west, from the general direction of Sutton's place. It was a tall man on a dark horse. As the form came closer, Clay decided the man wasn't Sutton; the man wasn't blocky enough. If the rider kept his course he would come within a half mile of Clay, cut across the creek behind him, and strike for the ford upriver. It was the way Clay would take to get back to the Cross Pole. He watched the rider approaching, not fast and not slow, half in shadow and half in sunlight. Then Clay recognized the hatbrim turned up in front, the lanky form of the rider, and the slate-colored horse. It was Highpockets.

Well, well, thought Clay. Good old Highpockets, on an errand of good will. Good old Highpockets, who acted as if he didn't have a secret in the world. In bunkhouse talk he could go on about the brush country south of San Antone, his kinfolk, and what a name Kress was in that country, and how he was named Oliver after an uncle who later died in the war. He laughed at Two-Dollar Bill, who even today might jump if someone came up behind him unexpectedly. Good old slow-walking Highpockets, who made like his life was an open book. Well, it was more open at the moment than he probably realized.

Clay put his hand over Rusty's nose and watched Highpockets angle away and dip out of sight. Then he put his foot in the stirrup and swung back on top. The sun was moving across the sky, and pretty soon the shadows would begin to stretch.

As Clay rode on, he got to thinking about Lupita. She was obviously not as stirred as he was, but there seemed to be a ripple of interest there. It had certainly gotten his own current flowing. He grinned. It felt like the real juice.

When he got to the place he checked first to see that the stakes were in place, and they were. Then he came back to the point where he had ridden in, the point where she would see it first. He wondered what she would think of it, this piece of grassland a half mile square. It would look bare to her until there was a house, and even then they would want to put in a few trees. But there was water – that was the good thing. A man could dry-camp or travel to water, but if he wanted to make a home, which meant a woman, they needed water. Water for the stock, of course, but more than that, water for the kitchen, the bathtub, the washtub, the garden. He thought of his visit earlier in the day, and he realized how clean everything had been – the house, the glasses and tableware, the clothes. That was a good image. He had seen

41

rag-tailed nester children and had thought that even if he lived in a sod shanty, his kids would be clean. He thought of Lupita, and everything was bright and clean.

As Clay thought of the Campos household, he remembered a comment of Two-Dollar Bill's. 'Them Mexicans stick together,' he had said. 'Blood's thicker'n water.'

Regardless of how Bill meant it, there seemed to be some truth in the saying from the way they held together as a family and, beyond that, as a little community. Maybe blood was thicker than water, but to follow it a little further, water counted for something. Tony and the others, including Lupita, he thought with a smile, had accepted him as a friend. He was the outsider, and they had taken him in as a fellow human being. If blood was thicker than water, water was still better than air. It seemed to Clay that no more than air existed between the dark-featured people and those like Two-Dollar Bill, who volunteered his bias, and Highpockets, who denied he had one.

Good old Highpockets. Clay could hear him squeaking, 'He's a Meskin, and he's a good 'un.'

Clay nudged his horse and headed for the creek. It was time to get a drink and head back. Highpockets had a good lead on them, so they could travel fast. Clay slipped out of the saddle and let Rusty drink. Then he pushed his hat back on his head and knelt upstream from the horse. As he lowered his lips to the water, he thought of Lupita as he had first seen her walking through the lamplight.

Whap! Something hit him on the back of the head, and his face dipped into the water. As he pulled back and opened his eyes, he saw his dove-colored hat in the water ahead of him and to his left, right-side up and starting to float. He grabbed for the hat, at the same time remembering that his gun was in the saddle-bag. As he turned in a crouch, with his eyebrows and mustache dripping, he saw that the horse had jumped aside. He turned around farther, and standing there coiling his rope was Alex Thode.

Thode laughed. 'Don't let your shadow hit the water, boy. You'll scare the fish.' Thode was obviously pleased with himself for sneaking up with his shadow behind him.

Clay had regained his senses enough to look at Thode's face in the afternoon sunlight. The whole left side was puffed up and splotched purple and black, with an underhue of greenish yellow as the sun hit it. The swelling gave his cheek a twisted look, almost closing off the bloodshot eye that was set back in like a ruby. That was what Lupita had seen – a face that looked like a pan of rotten meat. Even Clay, who had seen a few messes in his time, found it sickening to look at.

It must have shown on his face. Thode sneered at him and said, 'Looks pretty, doesn't it?'

Clay stood up and said nothing. He wondered if Thode was alone. Maybe he had ridden a ways with Highpockets and then come up on Clay like a duck hunter on a pond.

'I said, looks pretty, doesn't it? Or don't you understand English?'

'If you weren't so smart with that rope, you wouldn't have to be so worried about how you look.'

'Smart? You'll find out how smart it is to put your hand on another man's rope.'

'Throw it again and see what happens, now that my back's not turned.'

Thode spat. 'Piss on you!' he said, moving the rope to his left hand. That left his right hand free, and he was wearing a gun. Clay noticed that Thode was neat and clean as usual, down to the clean vest and gloves.

'Take your gun off so you don't get it dirty,' Clay taunted, 'and we'll go at it. Gentlemen's rules.'

'Piss on you!' Thode said again. 'You give me a week,' he said, and his voice seethed as his chest rose. He raised the coiled rope with his gloved left hand. The hand shook as he pointed toward his bloodshot eye, and the rope coils trembled. 'When this goes down we'll go at it, anybody's rules.'

Clay thought for a moment. Thode couldn't shoot him for no reason, especially if he was unarmed, and Thode didn't want to fight. So Clay asked, 'Then what do you think you're doing today, swingin' your rope?'

Thode put on a justified air. 'I came to tell you to stay off the Silver Plains range.'

'What do you mean?'

'This is all Silver Plains Land and Cattle range, and if you knew

43

what was good for you, you'd stay north of the river.'

Clay tried to stay cool. 'I think you're off your range yourself, right here. I filed a claim on this place a little over a month ago, and I've got papers on it. Or you can ride down to the Land Office in Cheyenne and look it up.'

Thode looked at him as if he were a fool. Apparently he had gotten a better hold of himself and had decided to talk down to Clay. That would give him an easier way out. 'You're kind of thick-skulled, aren't you? I told you this is Silver Plains range. All the land along both sides of this creek, and the stream back that way, too' – he jerked his free thumb back over his right shoulder, to the east – 'has all been taken. Maybe you have your map upside down.'

'I know where I am,' Clay said, 'and I know which way is up. As long as I'm within these four stakes I'm on my own place – which, as a matter of fact, you are too.'

Thode looked back over his left shoulder and whistled. Clay expected to see Sutton or a handful of Silver Plains waddies come over the rise, but instead he saw the palomino horse. It came trotting with its head off to the left, trailing the reins to the side so not to step on them.

'I'm goin' to tell Mr Sutton that he has a problem here,' Thode said as he gathered the reins.

'You can tell Mr Sutton what I told you.'

'When Mr Sutton has a problem,' Thode answered, ignoring Clay's remark, 'he deals with it. I'll tell him about this, and I'll tell him you've been warned.' Then he turned his back to Clay, mounted the palomino, and kicked it into a lope.

He's a coward, Clay thought. *He doesn't know how to act on his own, not in this country. He backed off, even though he probably rode away pleased for knocking off my hat.*

Clay's mouth was dry. He went back to the stream and finished the drink of water that had been interrupted. Now there was more to think on. It was no wonder Sutton had made the offer to hire him. It wasn't out of regard for Clay's cowpunching abilities; it was to get his land. If Sutton's other cowboys claimed land and turned it over to the boss, then it made sense that Sutton would have liked to work a deal with Clay, to bring this parcel into the ditch project. It would be like Sutton to use his leverage as boss to get the land from a hired hand. He could lean on him to get what he wanted. From Sutton's point of view, Clay would then be free to claim another homestead, and no harm done. But then Clay had stumbled on to the scene by the river – and queered the deal, as the saying went.

Thode and Sutton were used to bullying Mexicans and getting away with it, and then Clay showed them up in front of a Mexican – and a sheepherder to boot. Clay decided he had been right in assuming that the job offer had gone void, and now he realized that he had goaded Sutton into a tougher line of action to try to get the land. It seemed pretty clear now. Clay's stomach tightened. Sutton would do what came easily to him anyway: use force. Or, as Highpockets would say, he would poosh, and poosh hard.

Highpockets had no doubt been over to the Silver Plains headquarters to tell what he knew and maybe to carry back a message. Thode had probably ridden partway back with him. Clay frowned. He didn't like having let Thode sneak up on him. He had let his guard down after he saw Highpockets go by – that, and he'd been thinking about Lupita and his visit.

Clay wondered again if Thode had ridden out with Highpockets. Probably so. And if so, maybe they had both seen him first, after all. If they had seen him, the lanky cowpuncher might have been acting as a decoy so Thode would know where to find his duck. Then, in turn, it would have been harder for Thode to shoot him, if the third man knew where they both were. Clay could bet he wouldn't find out from Highpockets himself, not the old poker-faced scout who never played poker.

CHAPTER 6

On the way back to the Cross Pole, Clay decided not to bring up any details about his visit to Mexican town unless he was asked. Naturally, he wouldn't say anything about seeing Highpockets or facing off with Thode. Depending on how things went, he might let Jamie in on it, but he wouldn't pass any remarks publicly.

When Clay rode in from the day's work on Monday evening, he saw they had what amounted to a new pet in the bunkhouse. Peck had hired a greenhorn kid who hoped to make a hand. Since roundup was still a little over a week away, there was time for him, in Bill's words, to get a little shit on the outside of his boots.

The greenhorn's name was Henry Thomasson, but it was evident from the beginning that he was going to be called 'the kid.' He was slender and soft-muscled yet, with a young face, plain blue eyes, and soft, light-brown hair. Highpockets had taken him under his wing, something like a hen with a duckling. He led the kid to a bunk, showed him the washroom, and pointed to the cookhouse next door. Clay smiled when he heard the older man assure the kid, 'We're just like family here.'

After supper the kid got his first lesson in manners, which in a way helped the condition of his boots. He asked Jamie Bellefleur why he had blond hair and a French name.

'I don't mind telling you,' Jamie answered, 'but you'd better learn not to ask personal questions. In my case it's nothing I'm touchy about. My father's family was French and my mother's family was Irish.'

'Oh.'

'But as a general rule, you'd do better not to ask that kind of question. If you listen, you'll learn as much as you're likely to find out from a man.'

'Well, thanks. I'm sorry. I didn't know—'

'That's all right. You're learnin'.'

'Well, I'll tell you what,' said Two-Dollar Bill, 'Peck puts on one more hand, and we'll have enough for a poker game.'

'How many does it take?' asked the kid. Then he looked around, as if embarrassed.

'That's an all-right question to ask,' offered Jamie. 'You usually like to have five or more. But with you we've still got only four, because Highpockets doesn't like the game.'

'But I'll tell you, kid,' said Bill, with a twinkle, 'I'll learn ya how to play Indian poker.'

'Indian poker? Is that something you do to greenhorns?'

'Hell, no. It's a card game. Also called Mexican Sweat. It's a game for only two. You need to know it if you get stuck in a line shack with another hand that don't know no other games.'

'You're not makin' fun of me?'

'No, I tell you it's a card game. A two-handed game.'

The kid looked at Jamie, who said, 'He's not makin' fun of you. It's really a game.'

Two-Dollar Bill and the kid then took their seats at the table, and the old hand explained to the kid how to play the game. Each player took a card off the deck without seeing it and held it against his forehead so that the other player could see it. Then a person bet on whether he thought he could beat the other card, and judging from his opponent's bets, tried to get a sense of the value of his own card. If one player had an ace or a face card, the hand didn't last very long. But if both players had low cards, the chips (or in this case, beans) might fly. Highpockets seemed to enjoy watching.

While the kid's education was progressing, Clay thought about drawing Jamie outside and telling him about Highpockets and Thode. Then, as he pondered it, he thought better of it. He didn't want to put Jamie in the position of taking sides. That was what happened sometimes when one puncher talked behind another's back. A man had to know that the other man thought the same as he did before he brought him into confidence. Clay had reason to believe Jamie didn't trust Highpockets, but that was it.

In less than an hour, all of the kid's beans had gone to the other side of the table. The kid went back to his bunk and stretched out, apparently determined to keep his mouth shut and listen.

After a little silence the talk picked up about the work coming up – roundup, haying, and then fall roundup and shipping. Naturally the older hands declared that it wasn't like it used to be. There was more haymaking and fenced pastures, and a man slept in his bunk damn near as much as he slept out on the ground. Next thing you knew, said Bill, they'd all be leanin' on fence posts, watchin' the neighbors. Then it would be time to move on, he said, and leave the land to the punkin rollers.

'What's a punkin roller?' asked the kid.

'A sodbuster,' said Bill. 'A dirt farmer.'

'Oh.'

'Dangerous man with a shovel,' Bill went on. 'I've heard of 'em standin' on a ditchbank, hittin' each other with shovels, fightin' over the water.'

'They do that,' said Highpockets.

'Ir-ri-ga-tion,' said Bill. 'Things'd be a hell of a lot better if they'd leave the country alone and not try to bring water to it.'

'There's water here,' said Highpockets.

'My ass,' Bill snapped back. 'I've rode this whole country from way north of here all the way to Texas, and way east to the old cow trails, and the big fact of this whole country is there's damn little water and a hell of a lot of land in between.' Bill raised his eyebrows as if to say, 'What do you think of that?' and began to roll a cigarette.

'Mind you, I'm not takin' their side,' Highpockets said, 'but they're just tryin' to use the water that's here.'

'Oh, you just been talkin' to Sutton too much.'

Clay watched as Highpockets stiffened, pursed his lips and licked them, then said, 'You'll hear the same from any of 'em.'

Bill raised his eyebrows again and lit his cigarette.

Jamie, who was good at smoothing the waters, spoke up. 'How do those ditch projects work?'

Highpockets sniffed, then said, 'You mean the private ones?'

'Uh-huh.'

'Well, they start with some capital and then try to get a grant or patent for, say, a million acres. There's got to be a stream in there, of course, and the bigger the better. Then they put in a dam and make a reservoir, cut their big ditches, and work it on down. Then they sell the land with irrigation rights to the farmers.'

Bill joined in. 'And then when the farmers go bust, the corporation buys the land back at two bits an acre and turns around and sells it to the next sucker. And that's when it's on the up-and-up.'

Highpockets looked at Jamie. 'You asked me how it works. That's the general idea of it.'

Jamie nodded. 'Is that what Sutton has in mind to do here?'

'Something like that, I would imagine. But I don't have any way of knowing.'

'I think they should just leave things be,' Bill said.

'I know how you feel, Bill,' Highpockets squeaked. When Highpockets talked fast or got contentious, the pitch went up as it did now. 'I'm not what you'd call a man of the future, but you can't fight progress.'

'You damn sure cain't,' said Bill. 'That's why me 'n' the kid're pullin' out as soon as he's old enough to shave. That right, kid?'

'Yep.'

'Bill, I bet you're still in this country after I'm gone,' Highpockets said in the same high voice.

'I wouldn't bet on it. And I'm a gamblin' man.'

It seemed to Clay that Two-Dollar Bill was even a little livelier than usual because he had the kid to entertain. It seemed especially so when after a short silence Bill said, out of the blue, 'Say, Highpockets, what time are them wimmen comin' by?'

'About the same time they always do.'

'You married, kid?' asked Bill.

'I think he's asleep,' Jamie said.

The talk of women did come around again the next night, and not entirely for the kid's benefit. Two-Dollar Bill, back on the topic of how the country was going to hell, said that he would quit punching cows someday anyway and get married.

'You?' said Highpockets.

'Yes, me.'

'Who's the lucky girl?'

'That's yet to be seen, but one of these days I'll settle down.'

'What for?'

'Seems to work that way. A fella quits punchin' cows, he gets married – or, he gets married, an' he quits punchin' cows. One follers the other.'

Jamie joined in. 'Are you on the lookout for a widow that's well set up?'

'I 'magine they're pretty scarce and bein' herded pretty close.'

'You're always welcome to glance through my paper,' Jamie said, smiling. He sometimes received a matrimonial paper called *Heart*

49

and Hand, although he hadn't yet written to any of the women listed. Clay recognized that Jamie's offer was not without its humor, as Two-Dollar Bill ignored every kind of reading material.

'I'd just as soon meet 'em face to face.'

'Come right down to it,' said Highpockets, his voice in high pitch, 'there ain't many wimmen in this country.' His tone didn't suggest that he thought it was either good or bad, just stating a fact.

'Not white women,' Bill answered.

Clay's stomach kicked. He hadn't liked that side of Bill before, and he liked it less now. It was the kind of thing Bill said by reflex, and in his own mind he probably meant no harm by it. Clay expected Highpockets to say something back, but he didn't touch it.

'Well,' said Jamie, who naturally had a broader view of such things, coming from the Wolf River country, 'there's a lot of pretty Indian girls, and that's a nice little wife Jackson Mead has got.'

Clay nodded. Jackson Mead was a trapper and guide who lived in a dugout on Stone Creek. There was quite an age difference between him and his wife, but they had a couple of little kids and seemed to do well enough.

'That's fine for him,' Bill answered. 'I know them Indian gals are supposed to make mighty fine wives, and Mexicans too, but I wouldn't have one for my own wife.'

Jamie glanced at Clay, who turned his mouth down to say, don't bother. Then Clay remembered Artois, the Canadian, and realized Two-Dollar Bill was just one less to worry about with the dark-haired girls. It brought a smile.

'What do you think, Clay?' Jamie asked.

'Oh, I think it takes a big steer to weigh a ton.'

On Saturday night, Two-Dollar Bill wanted to take the kid to town 'to see the critter,' but the kid didn't seem very eager. Highpockets said to leave the kid be if he didn't want to go. So Bill and Jamie went to town. The boys had just gotten paid, and roundup was starting next week. Roundup would last five or six weeks with no time off, so Bill was primed to let the coyote howl. Clay thought it was just as well that the kid didn't go this time, as Bill could get pretty drunk. Jamie said he could 'side' Bill 'plumb fine,' so off they went.

Clay stayed at the ranch for roughly the same reason the others went to town. He wanted to use this last free Sunday to ride to Mexican town, and he wanted to be in good shape to do it. So he got a good night's sleep. In the morning he got washed up, put on a clean white shirt, saddled Rusty, and rode out.

It was another beautiful day in the young time of year. The sun was warm, and the air was fresh with a light breeze blowing. Clay was wearing a denim jacket and, as always, had his slicker tied on the back of his saddle. His six-gun was in the saddle-bag, since it always seemed to be in the wrong place anyway. Clay looked up. A couple of puffball clouds floated in the blue sky. He looked to the west. The sky was clear, but that didn't mean much beyond the moment. From spring to fall in this country a storm could blow up at just about any time, usually in the afternoon. But right now the day was bright and happy.

The meadowlarks were out, making music and probably eating bugs. Clay looked around him on the ground, and a few yards off the trail he saw a cactus blossom. He rode past it and looked down on the silky yellow flower, the first one he'd seen this season. He thought of Lupita. At a moment like this, it would be nice to have someone to share it with.

He didn't see any more prickly pear in bloom for the rest of the ride into town. At the river he stopped to dismount and to water his horse. Then he was across the plank bridge and into the little world of Mexican town. He turned down the second street and found the stuccoed house with the wagon in front of it. Between the wagon and the house was a young tree he hadn't noticed the week before. It was some kind of shade tree, about eight feet tall, and it was just leafing out. Tied to the little tree with about six feet of hemp rope was a little black and brown goat with floppy ears. As Clay dismounted, the goat made a sound like 'ben-heh-heh-heh.' Rusty nickered back to the goat.

Campos appeared at the doorway and said, 'Hello, partner. Come on in.' Then he said, 'You wanna water your horse?'

'No, thanks. I let him drink at the river before coming across.'

'Well, come on in.'

They sat at the table as before. Tony asked Clay what he would like, and Clay asked for coffee. Tony called to the kitchen, and in

51

a few minutes Clay had a cup of tan coffee in front of him. He didn't usually take milk in his coffee. He sipped it and it tasted good. Tony pushed the sugar bowl toward him, after taking two spoonfuls for himself. Clay added a short spoonful to his own.

They had been talking about the regular things – work and the weather – and they came to a moment of silence. Then Clay said, 'I ran into our friend Thode after I left here last week.'

Tony frowned and motioned toward the kitchen.

Clay nodded. He had noticed last time that Tony had changed the subject when Lupita was at the table. Clay imagined that Margarita must have told him in the meanwhile that their talk was overheard from the kitchen.

'It didn't amount to much anyway,' Clay said.

Tony said, 'Good.'

As they picked up the thread of conversation again, Tony asked Clay where he was from, if his folks were still alive, and if he had any brothers or sisters in this part of the country. In return, Clay asked him about himself. He learned that Tony and Margarita were from Sonora. They had come to the U.S. when they were young, to get away from troubles that her family had with another family. He went to work for the railroad and followed his work around the country until they settled here. He said he learned English with the railroad crews.

'All my boys are learnin' English,' he said. 'You gotta speak English. If two mexicanos are speakin' Spanish, well someone thinks they're talkin' about 'em. And it's better for makin' a livin'.'

Clay nodded. 'Yeah, people always think someone's talking about them.'

'Sure. If I'm sittin' in the Red Rose Saloon and I don't speak English, and you and some of your partners are talkin' and laughin', I'm gonna think you're talkin' 'bout me.' Tony drank from his coffee. 'No, I rather talk English – around white people anyway.' He laughed. 'Then they think you're a good Mexican.'

Clay laughed. 'Are you?'

'I guess so. There's different kinds of good Mexicans.'

As they talked on, Clay found himself getting anxious to see Lupita. He had been hearing two voices in the kitchen, along with the other sounds of chopping, clanging, and frying, but so far he had seen only Margarita. Eventually Lupita appeared with a handful of spoons and forks.

Clay's heart gave a happy little leap as his eyes met hers. 'Hello,' he said.

'Good afternoon,' she answered, smiling. As she set the utensils around the table, she asked, 'How do you like your goat?'

'You mean the little fella outside?'

She smiled and nodded, her face shining.

'I hope it's not for me,' he said, looking at her and trying to tell if she was joking. 'I don't have a place to keep him.' Then he thought of his hundred and sixty acres, and he added, 'Not yet, anyway.'

She looked at him with her lips almost in a pout and then said, 'You don't like him?'

Clay stammered, 'Well, yeah, of course I do.'

She laughed and went back to the kitchen.

Tony's face was lit up. 'I just got him yesterday.'

'He's a cute little fella,' Clay said. 'He talked to my horse, and my horse answered.'

'Horses and goats get along real good,' Tony said.

'I've heard that. I've heard that if you let a goat clean up in the barn where you grain the horses, he'll keep down the disease. Doesn't seem to be very popular out here, but I've heard it.'

'Oh, yeah. And a horse, a lotta times he's real nervous, you know, and a goat he's *tranquilo*.'

'Tron-kee-lo.'

'Uh-huh. *Tranquilo*. Calm. And you know if you got a little baby horse and the mother died, you get a goat.'

'For the milk?'

'No, you gotta feed him milk, but the goat keeps him company.'

'Really.'

'That's what they say. And it works.'

'What have you got in mind for this one?'

'We probably eat him in the winter.'

'Oh.'

Before long, dinner was on the table. There was rice and

beans, and chunks of chicken covered in a thick brown sauce called *mole*. The meal went as it had gone the week before – Margarita tending the table until the boys had finished.

Clay stole several sidelong glances at Lupita, who was wearing the same tan dress she had worn before. She was also wearing small, red, ovalshaped earrings that dangled on thin golden loops. He didn't remember seeing them before, and he was sure he would have noticed. They were a rich color and not too big – about the size of a small dry bean – and they went well with the dark hair and bronze skin. He noticed again the neat eyebrows and the long lashes as she bent to eat. Each time he looked at her he could feel the current flow in him, like a ripple.

As she was finishing her meal, he made his first try at holding her in conversation. He asked her about her week at the bakery, which didn't turn into much of a topic. Then he said, 'I was wondering what your full name is.'

She said, 'My name is Maria Guadalupe Fuentes Carrillo.'

'It sounds pretty the way you say it.'

'Thank you. Lupita is short for Guadalupe. We have two last names, you know, from our father and our mother. If we just use one, like we do here, we use the first one. So I am Lupita Fuentes.'

'Uh-huh. I think I followed that. Where do your parents live?'

'They aren't living anymore,' she said, looking down. Then she looked back up and said, 'That's why I came to live with my aunt.'

'Is she related to—'

'My father.' She held her two index fingers side by side. 'They were brother and sister.'

'I'm sorry you lost your parents so young.'

'It was very hard,' she said, 'but it was what God wanted.'

'You just try to make the best of it,' he said, realizing what he said wasn't exactly the same thing.

'Are your parents still living?'

'Yes.'

'Do they live here? You don't live with them if you work on a ranch.'

'No, they live in Oregon, along with my brother and my sister, about a thousand miles from here.'

'That's too bad. You must miss them.'

'I get along.'

She nodded. He imagined she understood him about as well as he understood the part about what God wanted. It made sense, but only from the outside.

They sat for a moment in silence, and apparently she wanted to cheer things up as much as he did.

'Did you like the dinner?' she asked.

'Oh, yeah. I like all food.' He smiled, and she smiled back. Then he had a thought. 'Do you like yellow?'

'Yellow? The color?'

'Uh-huh.'

'Well, yes.'

'I'll tell you, I saw the prettiest flower today. A yellow cactus flower. It was the only one I saw today, like that, anyway. I wish I'd brought it.'

She smiled. 'They're pretty.'

'Maybe I'll bring one next time,' he said, and then he realized he probably wouldn't see her again until after roundup, when all the cactus flowers would be gone.

'That would be nice' she said. Then, getting up, she said, '*Con permiso*. I'd better start washing the dishes.'

Clay yearned to keep her at the table to talk some more, but he could tell the visit with her was over – for today, at least. It hadn't been all happy and bubbly, but there was a warm undercurrent. As he reflected on the conversation, he was glad he mentioned the cactus flower. Even if he might not see her again for a while, he felt encouraged by the idea that there would be a next time.

As he left the Campos household a little later that afternoon, he saw the little goat on the ground with its legs folded underneath it. Its eyes were half-closed and it was working its lower jaw placidly. *Tranquilo*. It was a curious notion, that this animal could absorb all the troubles of another, keep it calm and healthy. Maybe it was an odd idea, but there was something to it or people wouldn't put stock in it. He thought about that for a little while, but by the time he had gotten over the bridge, put the town behind him, and was out on the open plains again, his thoughts were all about a yellow cactus blossom and a girl with red earrings and black hair.

CHAPTER 7

Two-Dollar Bill and Jamie Bellefleur had made it back to the Cross Pole on Sunday afternoon, so Bill was sober enough on Monday to turn out with the rest of the hired hands. As was Bill's style, he didn't give the slightest acknowledgment of a hangover even though, as Clay noticed, his fingers shook as he buckled on his spurs.

Peck came to the cookhouse in the morning and gave orders to get started with preparations for roundup. Bill and Highpockets and the kid would bring in the horses that hadn't been ridden all winter, while Clay and Jamie would get the wagons ready. A blacksmith was coming over from the Ten Mile outfit to help with the wagons and any other ironwork that needed to be done. Peck said he would line out each man with a string of horses the next morning. Then he said he was going to town for the day, and he was gone.

The Cross Pole took part in what was called a shotgun roundup. It consisted of riders from a handful of small outfits that banded together to form a full roundup crew. Each outfit supplied horses for its own riders, but they all moved together as a crew with only one chuck wagon and one wagon for the bedrolls. Peck was the roundup foreman, and the Cross Pole wagons would roll with the crew. In the couple of weeks before roundup, the blacksmith from the Ten Mile made the rounds of the other outfits to help them get ready.

The blacksmith showed up at midmorning in a wagon carrying his tools and a load of blacksmithing coal. He set up a forge in the lee of the harness shed and went to work. His name was Ferris, and he was a cheerful, husky, blond fellow in his late twenties. He had a knack for fixing things, and he understood machines. He could repair anything on a mowing machine or hay rake as well as any of the iron-work on a wagon. Branding irons and campfire tripods were child's play to him, and he enjoyed experimenting with various latching devices to snug up pasture gates made of poles and barbed wire.

Clay and Jamie made good time cleaning out the wagons, greasing the axles, checking the hardware, and giving Ferris a hand. By the end of the day the blacksmith had time to go through the hand tools to mend a shovel and straighten out a pitchfork, and by sundown he had his anvil and bellows and tools loaded up to roll out in the morning. Clay and Jamie left him leaning against the wagon, smoking his curved-stem pipe, as they went to the horse corral to see the herd the boys had just brought in.

The horses were milling and kicking up dust, but Clay could pick them out one by one and recognize them from the year before. He knew Jamie was doing the same. Each man would get three horses or so out of this bunch, plus the four or five he had been riding, to make up his string. Each rider had his own string of company horses, and it was considered his string. No one rode a horse out of another man's string without his permission, and a man was expected to saddle and ride all his own. If a horse was unbroke or an outlaw, it was up to that rider to make a workhorse out of him for the season. Clay counted the horses. There were twenty-two just brought in. The Cross Pole usually brought five riders and provided the night wrangler, so to fill out all those strings, including the foreman's string and a couple of gentle horses for the kid, they would use just about all of the rough stock. Clay figured the kid would be night wrangler, which was usually a greenhorn's job, and he imagined Peck would bring back another regular hand from town.

Just before supper, Peck returned in the buckboard. He had another hired man with him, who got down from the wagon with his war bag. Clay could see him through the open door of the bunkhouse. He seemed unsteady, as a person is apt to be after sitting on a wagon seat for hours and then trying out his land legs. When the man got to the doorway, however, he looked as if he hadn't been eating well and hadn't come fully around from a rough winter. He was lean and pale, clean-shaven, with bloodshot nose and upper cheeks. His pale brown eyes were glassy and tired looking. Clay imagined he was about the same age as Two-Dollar Bill but much the worse for wear. He smiled at the idea that the man could have been sent from the Lord as a living lesson for Two-Dollar Bill to avoid the demon whiskey.

'Name's Slim,' said the man, looking around with his tired eyes. 'Peck put me on for the roundup.'

Clay showed him to an empty bunk, then took him to the washroom and through it to the cookhouse, where he introduced him to Mulkey the cook. Mulkey told them to go ahead and sit down, as he was going to beat the triangle in a minute or two anyway.

Slim was neither friendly nor unfriendly as the supper table filled up. He ate without talking, tossed his plate and silverware into the wreck pan, and went back to the bunkhouse. When Clay and the others, including Ferris, got back a little while later, Slim was already asleep. Well, thought Clay, don't judge a man till you've seen him ride, but from the looks of those horses out in the corral, tomorrow might be a long day.

Slim looked steadier in the morning, and when Peck gathered the men at the corral, Slim had a rope and looked like business. Peck's method was to point out the horses for each man's string and then let him work with the horses for two days before the outfit rolled out.

Peck looked over the men and saw they were all there. He looked at Clay and said, 'Clay, you stand by till I get the rest of them lined out.'

Clay nodded and stood by to watch and listen as Peck assigned horses. He gave Highpockets four of the most manageable. Then to Jamie and Slim he gave each a mix of two rough horses and two that weren't so bad. After the three men had each roped a horse and led it away, Peck spoke to Two-Dollar Bill.

'Bill,' he said, 'I want you to help this boy. He's gonna have to ride a couple of green-broke horses. We can't baby him if he wants to make the grade.'

Two-Dollar Bill stuck out his lower lip and nodded. He kept track of the horses as the foreman called them out, and then he led the kid through the corral poles and roped out a horse.

By Clay's count, there were only six horses left, and not all of them peachy.

Peck looked at Clay with his hazel eyes, eyes that never looked the same color twice. 'Clay,' he said, 'I'm makin' you the night wrangler.'

Clay felt as if he'd been kicked in the stomach. Night wrangler was the lowest job on the roundup, and it would be humiliating for anyone who could rope and ride. For someone who had been a regular hand with the outfit for three years, it was an insult. 'Night wrangler?' he said.

'Yep. I know it might seem like gettin' lowered a notch, but we're a little shorthanded. And I want Bill to make a hand out of that kid.'

Clay couldn't believe it. Hire two new hands, a greenhorn and a drunk who's just drying out, and make a night-hawk out of a regular hand? He felt himself starting to get mad, starting to pump up. A man wasn't supposed to talk back, but he said, 'Why are you putting me there?'

Peck looked at the milling horses. 'I need a good man at every job,' he said. 'Now, I'm gonna give you that blue roan and the white horse standin' behind it. They're gonna need some work, but I know you can do it.' Then Peck walked away without looking back at him.

Clay was furious. He could feel it in his stomach. He could feel it in his arms. The roan was a vile little horse, a biter and a kicker on top of his other tricks. They hadn't even taken that horse out on fall roundup last year. The white horse wasn't mean, but he had an outlaw streak in him that came out without warning, and in the middle of a calm ride he would take to pitching and bucking. Two-Dollar Bill had said they should shoot him for bear bait.

These were Clay's horses. The ones he had been riding had probably been turned over to the kid. A damn fuzzycheeked kid who couldn't rope his own horse. Clay had an iron grip on the rope at his side. By God, if Alex Thode so much as touched his hat right now, he'd slap him with that rope, slap him silly, grab him by that leather vest and slam him to the ground, rub that purple face in the dirt.

A sharp call from the corral brought Clay out of it. It was Bill telling the kid to stand back. Bill had roped their second horse and was trying to stay straight in front of it, pulling down on the rope and leaning back flat-footed.

Work's work, Clay thought. He loosened his grip on the rope and crawled through the corral poles. He'd rope the roan first and try to keep the teeth in his mouth.

Clay knew to keep the roan snubbed close when he was saddling him, but the horse bunched his body forward and around and tried to bite Clay as he followed. Clay dropped the saddle and punched the horse in the side of the nose, feeling the wet velvet give. The agate eyes widened and the horse straightened out. Clay took a deep breath, picked up the saddle and blanket, and slung them on to the horse's back.

As he ran the latigo through the cinch ring, he thought about how this would look to the other punchers. Then there would be the men from the other outfits, too, who had worked roundup with him before. He would feel ashamed, degraded. His thoughts ran to Peck again. The man couldn't be thinking right. If he wanted to get his work done and get it done right, he'd have to see what a stupid move it was. Then he'd put the kid on night wrangler where he belonged, give Clay back his string, and get some cattle worked. Clay kneed the roan in the belly where the horse had blown up against the cinch, and he gave the latigo a yank. Night wrangler, on a wildcat and a spook horse. *Tranquilo*, my ass.

The night wrangler's job was to ride herd on all the roundup horses as they grazed at night. A night herder needed gentle, well-trained horses that knew the rounds and were calm and surefooted in the dark. Night herding on a shotgun roundup was even harder than with a single outfit because the horses didn't know each other and had different home ranges. There would be upward of two hundred horses, and a good night horse made all the difference. A thickheaded or ornery horse could make the work many times harder, and downright dangerous.

In addition to herding the horses at night, the night wrangler was to drive the bed wagon from one day's camp to the next, gather firewood, help the cook, butcher beef as it was needed, and make himself useful. If he got two hours' sleep underneath the wagon he was lucky, and no one worried if the nighthawk didn't get any sleep. On lots of nights he didn't. Just about the only time he got a decent sleep was when the crew didn't move camp. The more Clay thought about the job he'd been given, the more he thought the move was aimed at trying to get him to quit. But he couldn't imagine why, and he wasn't going to be a quitter. He wouldn't give someone else the satisfaction, and it just wasn't in him to quit.

Another person who wasn't pleased with Peck's strange move was Orin Mulkey, the cook. He had expected to get the kid as night wrangler, and he had already begun to break him in by bossing him around whenever the kid was in the cookhouse. Now he had to give orders to Clay, who had earned more respect as a cowhand than any night wrangler could expect until he moved up. Clay could tell that the cook was uncomfortable having him as a lackey, especially when the person who should be the underling was out of place as well.

Mulkey said to Clay, 'That's a hell of a way to break in a kid, teach him he don't have to work his way up. He'll have the wrong idea from the git-go.'

Mulkey had a clear sense of hierarchy. By tradition, the cook was second in authority in the cow camp, and the area around his chuck wagon was his domain. Mulkey had been a cowpuncher himself, but he got a bum leg for his efforts and learned to handle pothooks and Dutch ovens. He was hard-bitten and given to hard drinking. It was a firm rule that there should be no liquor on roundup, but no one would have checked his gear. He slept in the bed wagon on roundup and had his own boar's nest in the cookhouse the rest of the time; the men left him alone. He was easier to get along with that way. With his red hair running to gray, his green eyes, flushed face, and yellow teeth, he had the looks to go along with his disposition. Or, as Clay sometimes thought, it might be the other way around.

With Mulkey as his boss, Clay went to work loading the chuck wagon while the other hands, old and new, worked with the horses. Clay wondered how long he would really last if Peck didn't come to his senses, but he knew he could at least get along with Mulkey. The cook obviously knew something wasn't straight, but he didn't say anything more about it to Clay. He gave him work to do and some time to work with the two horses, and he didn't treat him like a kid.

The other four outfits came in during the day on Thursday, so the whole crew would be together when they rolled out the next morning. There was plenty of hand-shaking and laughter all around as old acquaintances were renewed and new ones were formed. Clay did not mix with the others as he ordinarily might have done. He felt ashamed at having his real job taken away from him, and he felt as if everyone he knew out on the range, with the exception of Ferris the blacksmith, was there to hear about it. Furthermore, he had to suffer it in silence, with no backtalk or even talking it over with someone else. Finally, just before the crew rolled out, Jamie Bellefleur, leading his horse, stopped to talk with Clay at the bed wagon.

Jamie did not speak very loudly, and the commotion around him made a good cover. 'I want you to know that I think you're being dealt a crooked hand here.'

'Thanks, Jamie.'

'Bill thinks so, too, but there's not a hell of a lot either of us can do about it.'

'Oh, no, I know that. It's my problem. But it's sure got me beat. I can't make sense of it.'

Jamie nodded. 'It's a puzzle.' Then he motioned his head toward Highpockets, who was sitting on the slate-gray horse about forty yards away with his lips pursed and both hands on the saddle horn. 'But I bet he's got a hand in it somewhere.'

Clay nodded. 'I wouldn't be surprised.'

Jamie looked at him and said, 'Well, good luck with it.'

'Thanks, Jamie. I appreciate it.'

Mulkey made camp early the first afternoon near Chokecherry Creek – or, as Highpockets would say, Chokecheery Crick. The crew made its first gather that day, and as Clay hauled water and firewood, the regular hands were branding the calves. A man on horseback would rope the calf, and a man on foot would throw it and sit on it. Then the calf would be branded and earmarked according to the outfit the mama cow belonged to, and if it was a little bull calf it was made a steer.

There was plenty of noise, with cows and calves bawling, men calling out warnings and instructions, horses heaving, and hoofs pounding. A wave of sadness washed through Clay as he walked past and caught the old familiar smells of dust, cow manure, and burned hair. Clay watched the hands at work. The kid was learning to flank calves and keep them down, and Slim looked like he was holding his own. It's not their fault, Clay thought.

That evening, just before chuck, Clay was surprised to see Alex Thode ride into camp with a Silver Plains cowpuncher and six more horses. Just before he went out for his first night with the horse herd, Clay caught word from the day wrangler that Thode had come to rep for Sutton, and the other hand had come along because Thode wouldn't have been able to get the horses there by himself. Also, Thode was already unhappy because he saw that the WD riders all had tents, little square tepees that slept two men each, and he was going to have to sleep in the open.

Clay scowled. Sutton had a right to send a rep, but it was unlikely that any Silver Plains cattle would be on the other side of the river and this far north. But it was a good job for Thode. A rep didn't have to take his two-hour shift at night-herding cattle, and he would get in plenty of roping.

Thode did just that. The next afternoon he roped over a hundred calves, and he wrote down the number in his own little tally book. It was evident right away that none of the other punchers cared for Thode. Even Highpockets was cool toward him. As for Peck, he didn't show one way or the other, but he did talk to Thode and treat him politely.

By the third day of roundup, Clay was feeling frazzled. He had gotten very little sleep in the daytime, and the nights had been one long struggle with the roan and the white horse. On top of that, Peck had had him butcher a beef that afternoon, a four-year-old heifer that had never taken the bull. Clay didn't mind butchering, but it was extra work and not easy. He had to gut and skin the animal on the ground, and each time he rose to straighten out his back, he would see Thode sitting pretty on his horse, or Highpockets talking to Peck.

Clay had his chuck quick and early before going on shift, and he was just eating his stewed dried peaches when Thode and a handful of others came in, got served up, and sat on the ground.

'Someone rode that black horse of mine,' said Thode, in a tone that could only be heard as accusing.

Clay glanced up.

Thode looked at him. The swelling had gone down, but the lower eyelid was still purple. 'I told you not to ever touch a horse of mine again.'

Clay told himself to stay cool. Maybe this was the whole reason for Thode even coming to their roundup. Clay looked straight back at Thode and said, 'As horse wrangler, I might have to touch a horse now and then. But I didn't ride one of yours and wouldn't. I wouldn't ride anyone's without their say-so.'

A voice came up from in back of Thode – Two-Dollar Bill's. 'Maybe it was someone else's horse. They all look so much alike.'

The other cowboys laughed. Thode said nothing. Clay got up and tossed his plate and hardware in the dishpan, exchanged a glance with Two-Dollar Bill, and dragged his feet out to the cavvy ground.

When Clay got to the herd he told the day wrangler, 'Thode's got a bug in his ass. He says someone rode his black horse.'

The other wrangler, a kid who had come with the Ten Mile outfit, spit on the ground. 'He's just making that up,' he said. 'No one's rode that horse.'

Clay spent a rough night on herd. A gentle horse would let a man snooze and still make the rounds, but each time Clay nodded off on the white horse he snapped back awake, afraid the horse might pitch him to be trampled by the others.

Sounds carried, and he was glad when he finally heard Mulkey clanking around the firepit. A little while later, as the sky was lightening in the east, the other wrangler relieved him and he straggled back to the campfire. He was working his way through his coffee and fried beefsteak when he saw Peck approach and stand over him: Peck in his early-morning manner. Clay wondered what low job he had for him today so he couldn't sleep.

Peck shifted his right boot, and Clay looked up.

'Westbrook, I've decided to let you go.'

Clay felt a jolt in the pit of his stomach. This was it. He looked at

Peck, who seemed to be looking right past him. 'What?' he asked.

'I'm lettin' you go.'

'Why?'

'I've got too many men, and I've got to let someone go.'

'So you're firing me.'

'That's the way it is.'

'Uh-huh.' Clay could see it. The kid would be night wrangler after all.

'You can go ahead and roll your blankets. You can take those two horses, one to pack your bed on, and turn 'em out when you get back to the place.' Then, with what was supposed to pass for generosity, he said, 'As a matter of fact, you can borrow one of 'em for a while if you need it.'

Clay was tired and dull, but not too far gone to feel further offended. 'No thanks,' he said. 'I'll get one somewhere else. And my blankets are already rolled.'

'You've got almost a week's wages coming,' Peck went on. 'This should cover it.' He handed Clay a ten-dollar gold piece. Clay was a forty-a-month rider.

If Clay had been standing up he might have punched the foreman, but as it was he just said, 'This is a damn poor way to treat a man, Peck.'

'You ought to be able to get on with another outfit. You're a good hand and everyone knows it.'

The outfits Clay could think of working for were all right there, being bossed by Peck at the moment. 'This is pretty poor,' he said, clenching his teeth.

'It's not like you've done anything wrong. You're not being blacklisted.'

'No, just fired.'

CHAPTER 8

Bt the time Clay had ridden back to the bunkhouse, gotten a few hours' sleep, and cleaned up, he had come out of his fog. He saddled his horse Rusty and rode out with the intention of borrowing another horse to pack his gear to the homestead. As he rode along, he tried to sort out what had happened.

It didn't take a Pinkerton detective to figure there was some kind of a triangle between Peck, Highpockets, and the Silver Plains. Clay started getting the bad treatment after Highpockets' visit to the Silver Plains, and then it got worse when Thode came to camp. Highpockets and Peck both seemed to be sidling up to Sutton, and now it also seemed as if Peck had been showing favoritism when he assigned horses. Highpockets, in turn, had probably been greasing the skids with Peck by reporting all the little things that went on among the cowpunchers. Sutton didn't have to return any favors, apparently. As the saying went, water flowed uphill toward money.

If Sutton and Thode were the source of his trouble, which seemed to be the case, Clay had to admit to himself that some of it was of his own making. If he hadn't butted into things that first time on the river, he wouldn't be looking for a packhorse. Then he smiled. He probably wouldn't have met Lupita, either.

Clay followed the trail toward town for a few miles, then struck a southerly course for the river. He intended to visit Jackson Mead at his dugout on Stone Creek. As a trapper and guide, Mead was sure to have a horse he could borrow. The older man was also levelheaded, and it might be good to have his view of things.

Jackson Mead was about fifty years old, with a full head of hair, a furrowed forehead, and sky-blue eyes. He went clean-shaven, as he had told Clay before, because his wife's people didn't like to have much to do with bearded white men. Dog faces, they called them.

Clay and the guide sat on the ground outside the dugout in the late afternoon sun. Mead had seen a good plenty of life, as he let people know early on, and now he was trying to paddle his canoe down the easy waters, with the help of a good wife. He had kept his hair while other men lost theirs, he would say, and he'd had run-ins with the government, the railroads, and the other big muck-a-mucks. Now he'd made things over and wanted to be left alone. All the same, he was a good listener and followed Clay's story with interest.

'Sounds like you're up against it,' he said. 'When these big bastards want something, they don't care about the little people. If they have to bribe someone in the state house, or bring in a hired gun, they'll do it. They'll burn a house to kill a rat, and they'll do anything they have to do to get away with it.'

'You think the main thing is my claim, then.'

'Seems like it. With Sutton, anyway. You ruffled their feathers by stickin' up for Campos. That has Thode on the warpath against you, which plays just right into Sutton's hand. Meanwhile the big man makes life miserable for you and tries to run you broke, hopin' you'll have to sell your claim, or move on, or both.'

'So to keep him off my back, all I have to do is give up my land.'

Mead smiled. 'And leave the country.'

'Well, I think I'll do just the opposite. I'm out of a job and don't have any place else, so I think I'll just camp on my homestead and start making my improvements.'

Mead nodded and smiled again. 'Just be ready to fight dirty. Meanwhile, go ahead and take a packhorse. And you better take a sheet of canvas, too, until you get a roof over your head.'

Even getting a camp set up was no easy job. After Clay had moved his bedroll, rifle, clothes, winter gear, and personal effects out to the place, he had to go back to Mead's and borrow an ax. He needed to cut poles to string up a makeshift tent. Leaving all of his belongings wrapped in a bundle in the middle of his quarter section, he hightailed it with Rusty and the packhorse.

Mead's dugout was six miles across country as the crow flew. It had been a long day since sunup that morning, from Stone Creek to the Cross Pole to the homestead and now back to Stone Creek. Clay made a short visit. He borrowed the ax, with a leather cover for the blade in travel, and he got back to the claim at dusk. From nearly a mile away he could see the white bundle on the prairie, like a baby wrapped in a blanket.

No one came by for the next few days as Clay got settled in. He pitched his camp, scraped out a firepit and lined it with rocks, and gathered firewood. With Rusty and a rope he dragged deadfall from the creek, and then at the camp-site he broke and cut the wood into lengths for the fire. He spent a little time each day hunting cottontails, and he wondered if anyone heard or paid attention to the gunshots. Thode was north of the river, as far as he knew, and Sutton's bunch should be out on roundup.

Clay had despised the ten-dollar gold piece that Peck had dropped into his hand, but now he was happy to count it in with his small savings. He was going to need a supply of grub and a few things to cook with, plus some tools. At the least he would need a shovel, some kind of pick or mattock, an ax, a saw, a hammer, and a brace and bit. After that he would see how much he had left to put toward a wagonload of lumber, a couple of rolls of tarpaper, and a keg of nails. Maybe Tadlock would carry him for some of that. He really had nothing, he thought, but a hundred and sixty acres and the drive to do something with it.

When Sunday came around, Clay cleaned up as well as he could at the creek. Sundays were the best time to visit Tony and Lupita. He secured his camp beneath the make-shift tent, saddled Rusty, and headed for town. As he thought about it, he realized he didn't need to go through town. He could angle across country, drop by and say hello to Jackson Mead, and follow the river to Mexican town. As he did so, he saw cactus blooming everywhere.

He knew he wasn't expected at the Campos house, but he also remembered Tony telling him that it was always his house and he was always welcome there. Therefore, without ceremony he rode up to the stuccoed house, tied his horse to the wagon, and knocked at the door.

Tony came to the door, blinking as if he had just gotten up from a nap. 'Hey, partner,' he said, giving Clay his hand, 'I didn't expect you today.'

'I had a change in plans.'

'Good, good. Come on in and sit down.'

Clay glanced towards the kitchen, once he had sat down and taken off his hat.

'They went to buy an errand,' said Tony.

'You mean they went on an errand?'

'Yeah, to buy food.'

'Well, I'll tell it quick then.' Clay told the story of losing his job, giving a general sketch of Peck and Highpockets.

Tony said, 'Well, at least you didn't get in no trouble. No fights or nothing.'

'That's true.'

'Well, you know, there's lotta work. It's not so bad.'

Clay then told him of his plan to put up a shack on his homestead, to prove up on it and keep any land grabbers and claim jumpers off of it.

'You got a quarter section, huh?'

'Yeah.'

'Probably you still have to work.'

'I think so. If I can get something established now, to keep everyone off it, then maybe I can get on with some outfit for the fall roundup, and I might even land something for the winter.'

Tony nodded. 'That's pretty good, to have that land. But you gotta be careful.'

'I can't just quit and let 'em take it.'

Tony shook his head. 'No, you can't do that.'

At that point the two women came in, each carrying a bulging cloth shopping bag. Margarita smiled and said good afternoon, then moved on to the kitchen. Lupita paused and took off her shawl as she spoke to Clay.

'I'm surprised to see you. You said it might be a month.' She smiled and gave him her hand. It was warm and dry, with a faint pressure in response to his.

'I had a little change in plans.'

'How nice. My aunt and I are going to cook *chile colorado*. Do you like it?' Her eyes met his.

Clay was happy. 'Sure . . . I don't know if I've ever eaten it. But you know I like all food, especially here.'

She said, 'Good. It's really delicious. But you don't want to eat too much. Some people, it makes them sick, a little too much.'

Clay grinned. 'I'll be careful.'

'Well,' she said, 'I better help my aunt. Excuse me.' She went to move on, and then she turned back to him and said, '*Con permiso.*'

'*Con permiso*,' he repeated.

The dish they called *chile colorado* was cubed beef swimming in a red chile sauce. He learned that *colorado* meant red, or colored.

69

It was a spicy dish, red hot with a strong undercurrent. It promised to give heartburn or worse. Tony told him that two helpings wouldn't hurt him but more than that would.

'Keep you up all night,' he said.

'Oh.'

After the dinner had been cleared away and Lupita still sat at the table, Clay decided to make his bold move.

'You remember last time I said I might bring you a flower?'

Her eyes sparkled as she smiled and nodded. 'Yes.'

'Well, the country's full of 'em right now, but they're kind of hard to pick.'

She seemed to see some seriousness in that. 'Yes, the little—' She paused for the word, tapping her index finger on an imaginary thorn. Then she said, 'Spines?'

'Thorns,' he answered. 'Or needles.'

'Oh, yes. Needles.'

'Well, anyway, since it's hard to bring the flowers to you, I thought I could offer to bring you to the flowers. Go on a little walk.'

She looked at the table. 'I barely know you.'

'Did I say something wrong?' Clay looked at Campos, who was staring at the sugar bowl.

'No,' she said. 'But I'm a little bit embarrassed. With my uncle sitting right here, it's his house, you know, it's hard to talk about it.'

'Should I wait?'

Lupita looked at her uncle.

'Marcos can go with you,' he said.

Clay realized at that point that it would have been much better if he could have contrived some way to take her aside and ask her. Then she could have asked her uncle according to form, he could have given permission, and he and Clay would not have had any contact over it. This was serious and mildly funny at the same time. He didn't think he'd offended anybody, no one had had to resort to Spanish, and he was going to get to go on the walk, but he wouldn't make that mistake again.

Marcos was the oldest of the four boys, the one who had fetched the beer in the cream can during Clay's first visit. Clay thought Marcos might like to ride the horse, and he was right. So they set out, Clay and Lupita on foot and Marcos on Rusty. Clay wondered what Two-Dollar Bill would think of it, to see a cowpuncher walking while a Mexican rode his horse.

Clay smiled to himself. He liked walking next to Lupita. She was very womanly, in her black shawl and light blue dress, her smooth features, her long dark hair, and her shapely body. Clay guessed her age to be about twenty-one. She had grown past the young, green age of girlhood but had the bounce and beauty that a man looked for in a young woman. Clay had known young women, and girls, who didn't like to walk in the country because of the dirt, the bugs, and the stickers. But Lupita seemed comfortable as she walked along the shortgrass prairie with Clay.

His design was to take her to the top of the bluff, about a mile from her house, so he could show her the river below and the country beyond. As they climbed the bluff, she laid her left hand on his right forearm in some of the steeper places.

There was a mild breeze blowing when they came out on top. She put back the shawl and let the wind riffle through her hair.

'This is pretty,' she said. 'I haven't been up here before.'

'It sure is. It's one of those pretty places you like to share with someone else.'

She nodded.

'I think the river looks magical from here, don't you?' he said. 'It's one river, then two rivers, then one river again. The Indians called this place Twin Rivers.'

'Really?'

'That's what I've heard.'

'It's such a pretty thing to see.'

Clay turned to check on Marcos, who was shading his eyes and peering at the river. Then he turned back to Lupita. 'You see over there? Off in that direction, about eight miles in a straight line, or maybe a little less, is where my place is.'

'The ranch where you work?'

'No, that's off to the north.'

'That's what I thought. Then what place is that?'

'It's my homestead. It's a hundred and sixty acres that's mine if I take care of it.' He paused to see if she was following, and then

71

he went on. 'That's where I'm living now.'

'I thought you lived at the ranch.'

Clay felt a pang of sadness. He had an image of Jamie and Two-Dollar Bill roping calves at that very moment. 'I used to,' he said. 'But I don't work there anymore. That's why I could come and visit today.' He choked out the words. 'I got fired.'

'Fired? Really?'

'I think the foreman did it because he wanted to get in good with the bigwigs your uncle and I ran into down over there.'

'That's too bad.'

'Uh-huh.'

They stood for a long moment without talking. Then she asked, 'Have you been in a lot of trouble?'

'No, not really. Not until this mess. Why?'

'You seem so serious.'

He gave a half-laugh. 'Life made me that way.'

'You just said this was the only trouble you had.'

He hesitated. Then he said, 'Well, about five years back I took a pretty big fall.' He looked off to the distant west. 'This girl I was crazy about, she up and married this other fella. It still makes me sick.'

'Five years? That's a long time.'

'Sometimes it seems like a long time, and sometimes it seems like yesterday and today.'

'But it's in the past.'

'It should be, but it comes creepin' up on me, and then it feeds into this other thing with Sutton. . . .'

'Is that the rich man?'

'Yeah. The one who started the trouble down there and probably got me fired.'

'My father was like that.'

Clay felt an alarm go through him. 'You mean a big shot?'

'No, I mean always having trouble.'

'Was he part of the blood feud?'

'The what?'

'The, uh – the fight with the other family.'

'Yes, and he was always worrying that someone was after him and was going to kill us all.'

72

'Always looking over his shoulder.'

She had her mouth set, and she just nodded.

'Is that how he died?'

'No, after all his worrying and my mother worrying, he was working on a windmill and he fell off.'

'Just fell off?'

'He didn't see it, and the tail came around and hit him.'

'And your mother?'

'She just worried and worried. Always nervous. I don't want to be like that. She died about a year later, and I came to live with my aunt. My cousins were married, and my aunt needed help.'

'How long ago was this?'

'About four years.'

'And your father just had that one trouble?'

'Yes, but he always had it. It stayed with him and followed him.'

'That's too bad. . . .'

'That's why we like it here. The rest of our family is a long ways away, but we don't have any trouble.'

Clay decided he'd try to cheer things up. 'Cactus flowers are sure pretty, aren't they?'

She looked at the ground near her feet, where a pair of blossoms smiled up at the young couple. 'Yes,' she said. 'They are.'

'I've got a million of them on my place,' he said.

She looked out in the distance where he had pointed earlier.

Then he said, 'I'd like to show you my place sometime.'

She looked at Marcos, sitting on top of the horse and smiling. She laughed.

Clay laughed, too. 'Yeah, it would be a long walk.'

When Clay got back to his cactus garden at sunset, everything was as he had left it, except for a rattlesnake coiled up on his bedroll. He prodded the snake out of the tent and killed it with the ax. Then he rolled out his bed and crawled in.

She had said she barely knew him. That meant they couldn't be very familiar. A kiss was still a ways off. For Clay it also meant he had time to show her that he wouldn't always have trouble following him.

CHAPTER 9

On Monday morning Clay dug out a pencil and paper and drew a diagram of the shack he planned to build. With that he could figure the lumber he would need, and then he could go into town. Knowing that he was going to have to build it by himself and live in it by himself, he decided to make it small and manageable. He knew that an eight-by-fifteen shack was no place to ask a woman to come and live, but it would do until he got this trouble worked out.

If he was going to settle on a piece of land, that meant home, which in turn meant a woman someday. He smiled to himself as he remembered Two-Dollar Bill's formula.

Getting married and quitting the cowboy life were supposed to go together, but he wasn't sure he was through punching cows, whether he settled down or not. Even as the country changed, there would be work. It was many a man's dream to have a spread big enough to make a living, and a hundred and sixty acres of grass wasn't going to do it. But it was a place where he could feel free – free within boundaries – and it was a place to make a life. Eventually that life would include someone else.

Clay thought of the men he knew who were older than himself, and he could see which ways the trail forked. There was Two-Dollar Bill, who said he would settle down but seemed to be stuck in a pattern of living from payday to payday. There was Mulkey, who showed where a fellow could end up if he just stayed a hired hand and things went as well as they had gone for the cook. As for boss jobs, there simply weren't that many. If a fellow kept on as a bunkhouse hand he was liable to stay single, which would make for a lonely life – unless, of course, he was like Highpockets, which Clay wasn't. And then there was Jackson Mead. Clay didn't intend to wait that long to settle down with a family, but he hoped he had something like a family when he was

74

in middle age. It was a world better than beating the triangle and bullying the wrangler.

He had never really doubted that someday he would settle down with a woman, but it was an idea that had always been off in the distance. Now that he was on his own place, the idea came closer, especially since he'd felt the first blush of tender feelings for Lupita. But maybe the idea was coming close too quickly. The old trouble with Rosalind still kept coming to mind. He knew deep down that Lupita was different. She was quieter, deeper – truer, really. If things developed with her, he would not have to doubt or worry. There would be trust. But he didn't know if he was ready for it. He had trusted before and had been devastated. He was getting better, but as much as he was attracted to Lupita, he didn't know if he was ready to take the plunge.

No hurry, thought Clay. *Tranquilo.* He could get things nailed down here, get Sutton and Thode off his back if he could, go back to working for wages, and build up some savings. It was a matter of keeping cool, staying out of trouble. Tony was right – and there was a happy man with a family. Anyway, Tony was right. Clay had lost his job, but at least he hadn't gotten into any more trouble over it.

Through the open end of his shelter he saw a rider coming. He laid down the pencil and paper and pulled his rifle out of the scabbard where he had it cached in his pile of winter clothes. Whoever it was, he was coming from the direction of Silver Plains.

The rider came closer. Not big enough to be Sutton. Not bright and shiny like Thode. The rider came closer yet. To Clay's surprise, it was Jamie Bellefleur. Clay wondered if he had gotten fired, too, or – less likely – if he had gone to work for Silver Plains. Clay put the rifle back in place and went out to meet him.

'Top of the mornin',' Jamie said as he rode up.

'I didn't expect to see you,' said Clay. 'They didn't fire you too, did they?'

Jamie laughed. 'No, I'm a company man,' he said as he dismounted.

As they shook hands, Clay could tell he had nothing to worry about from this visit, although he had been apprehensive at first. 'Well, tell me about it. I wish I had some coffee to offer you, but I'm plumb out. I was just gettin' ready to go to town.'

'That's all right,' said Jamie. 'I had plenty at Sutton's bunkhouse.' He seemed to be amused, and the scar above his eyebrow danced.

Clay made a motion, and they both sat on the ground. 'Is that right? What took you there?'

'Oh, I had to help our little partner Thode get his horses back across the river.'

'He left the roundup?'

'Uh-huh. He stayed a little over a week. There was damn little for him to rep, anyway. After he got his bed rained on a couple of times he decided to pull out, and Peck sent me to help him bring his horses back.'

Clay smirked. 'Did he get to rope plenty of calves?'

'Yes, he did. And I think he got every one of 'em accounted for in his little tally book.' Jamie chuckled.

'Well, good for him. And how's the kid?'

'Just fine. Went to night wrangler, of course.'

'Of course. Is Mulkey bringin' him up right?'

'Seems to be.'

'And how about Slim?'

'He's a hand, but no great shakes.'

Clay thought for a moment, then said, 'So Peck goes shorthanded, sendin' you off, just to do a favor to Thode?'

'Or Sutton, seems like. I doubt Peck likes Thode any better than the rest of us do.'

Clay shook his head.

Jamie said, 'We were shorthanded enough when you left, and now me. I was gone all of yesterday, and I'll be a good part of today gettin' back.'

'And Peck said he had too many men. Said that was why he was lettin' me go.'

'Sure, he said that, but from what I gathered, Highpockets told him you were a troublemaker.'

'Highpockets, uh?'

'Yeah, or Ass-Pockets, as some of the other boys call him.'

Clay laughed. 'I'll tell you a little story about him. You remember the day I rode into town with you and Two-Dollar Bill?'

'Sure.'

'Well, I came by here on my way home, just to take a look at things, and who do I see headin' home but old Highpockets.'

'Makes sense.'

'Not long after that I ran into Thode, right here on my place.'

'Any trouble?'

'Not much. He knocked my hat off with his rope, but he wouldn't fight. Said he'd wait till his face got better.'

'Too bad you couldn't have whipped his ass.'

'He doesn't want to fight me one-on-one.'

'Nah.'

Clay paused for a moment. Then he asked, 'Well, what do you think is Highpockets' angle?'

Jamie pursed his lips, then spoke. 'The way I see it, he thinks Sutton is gonna buy up or grab up the whole country and he's hoping Sutton'll have a chair by the fire for his helper Highpockets.'

'So there's a good chance that Highpockets was tattling to Sutton, then carrying a message to Peck to put the pressure on me.'

Jamie nodded. 'That fits.'

'But why would Peck play along?'

'I guess to stay on Sutton's good side. He probably thinks Sutton will have a huge outfit and he can help boss it.'

'Then Highpockets would go with him?'

'That, or Highpockets would like to move into Peck's job if Peck goes to Sutton's and he doesn't.'

'Highpockets couldn't be a boss.'

'He doesn't know that. And meanwhile he kisses up to both of 'em.'

'What do you think is the reason they were after me? Jackson Mead thinks that Sutton wants to own it all, and I'm in his way.'

'Probably so. You hear different things. Some of those punchers on roundup are farther away from it than we are, so to hear them tell it, Thode came out to help Sutton start a bank – and all that sort of thing. Personally, I think Thode came out to be a cowboy and lord it over on the real cowboys.'

'That seems right.'

'But as far as Sutton is concerned, general opinion is that he's gatherin' up land. He's got punchers takin' up claims along here, and he's workin' hard on the Courtland place. If you haven't seen him much around here, it might be because he's spendin' more time down south.'

'Did you get some of this from his own boys?'

'They don't talk much. Not to me.'

Clay let out a sigh. 'And what about his big ditch project?'

'Seems to be in the works. He won't get any million acres, but with what he can get his hands on there, and his other finaglin', and what he already has, he could be pretty big.'

'I don't imagine I'm the only one in his way, if it's that spread out. He probably has other bugs to squash.'

'I suppose.'

'But he wants it all his way.'

Jamie nodded. 'Seems like it.'

Clay thought for another long moment, looping back to pick up a stray thought that had crossed through earlier. 'Why did Peck send you instead of Highpockets?'

'Probably to avoid being too obvious. And I did see Highpockets and Thode chinnin' once in a while.'

Clay and Jamie talked on for a short while longer. Clay told of his plans to build a shack and hold his place and then go back to earning wages. He wanted to tell him about Lupita, but it just didn't fit into the conversation, and he wasn't really sure about the push and pull of his feelings anyway.

After Jamie had been there for about half an hour, he said he'd better be moving along. He and Clay got up from the ground and shook hands. Then Jamie checked his saddle cinch, swung on, and waved as he trotted away.

Clay went back into the tent. Through the other end he could see Jamie riding off to the north. He picked up his pencil and went back to figuring.

A while later, Clay saddled up and rode to town. He bought a supply of grub, a few things for cooking, and the hand tools he thought he'd need. Then he arranged for a wagonload of lumber on credit, and Tadlock agreed to haul the bulk of the camp supplies and the tools along with the building materials. The wagon arrived at about noon the next day, and when it was gone, Clay was alone on his land.

For the next week as he worked on his house, Clay saw no one else. It was slow work, leveling the timbers for the foundation, making all the cuts and notches with the hand saw, and continually having to walk to the other end of whatever he was working on to square or straighten or check for flush. It was bound to be a rough-looking shack no matter what, and it would probably be just a tack- and toolshed later on, but he wanted to do as neat a job as he could.

He worked on through Sunday, watching the sky and wondering if he would get drenched before he got the roof covered. So far he had been rained on only once, and that was an afternoon shower that was good for the grass but didn't do him any harm. He laughed as he thought of Thode sleeping in the rain. He remembered the wet days on roundup, trying to work cattle on slick gumbo, huddling by the campfire under Mulkey's canvas fly as the horses stood by in the rain with slickers draped over the saddles. He missed it, even those days when no one was happy. By and by, the sun always came out, the bedroll dried out, and the stars were back in the sky.

Finally he had the walls and roof together, the whole outside tarpapered, and the wooden floor nailed down. First-rate, he thought as he thumped his knuckles on a floorboard. A skunk couldn't get under there. Maybe mice or a rattlesnake looking for mice. Good place to hide his money in a tin in case he turned into a miser like Highpockets. He looked at the open doorway. What he needed now was a door and hinges. All the lumber scraps had been too small, kindling size, except for the two pieces he'd rigged up for shelves.

He had laid out the shack running east and west the long way to take less of the wind, although the wind could come from all sides. The doorway was on the east end, in the leeward side of afternoon rains. It also let in the morning sun, and it looked out in the direction of a pretty, dark-haired girl who liked cactus flowers. The thoughts of her kept coming back.

After he had moved his belongings into the house, he brought a bucket of water up from the creek and went about making his evening fire. He hadn't thought much about a bucket before, until he got into playing this long hand of solitaire. It gave a man time to think. Of all the tools he used in managing his new life, the bucket had taken him by surprise. A rifle could bark here and put meat on the ground over there. Sharp tools cut things up, like prairie sod or lumber. Hard, blunt tools could drive a nail or a wedge, to join or split. A bucket could hold water.

He had always taken a bucket for granted – he either had one or he didn't – until he came to this piece of ground with nothing to carry water. After he finished off a can of tomatoes he had something to boil a small ration of coffee, but for everything else he had to go to the water. As Two-Dollar Bill had said, the big fact of this country was the distance between land and water. Clay saw the fact up close now, even with the short distance between his camp and the creek. Water had no shape. You couldn't pick it up with your hands unless you were kneeling to drink, and then you'd better be quick. To get water from one place to another, unless it was ice, a man needed something to hold it and give it shape – a ditch, a pipe, or a container like a bucket.

When life got down to its simplest, that was the value of a bucket. It brought water to the hearth, so a person didn't have to go to the stream or well for every little need. Clay had thought before about bringing water to the fireside, but he hadn't thought much about how he would do it. Lots of people had a well with a pump right in the kitchen. That would work, especially this close to a stream, where good drinking water wouldn't be too far down. But before that, when things were at their most basic as they were now, a bucket did the job. He appreciated a bucket more than he ever had before, because now he saw what it could do and what it represented. A bucket could carry and hold water, give it shape; and water was caught up in everything a man and a woman would have together.

CHAPTER 10

By the time he had built his little house, Clay had a good pile of kindling but was low on firewood. He and Rusty spent most of one day roaming up and down the creek and hauling dead snags back to camp. That afternoon and evening he broke and chopped nearly half of it, and he was building on a woodpile once again. He had bought his own ax, and it was a pleasure to swing it.

In the morning when he went to the creek for water, he saw a magpie rise from some tall grass not thirty yards away. A man usually didn't get that close to a magpie, especially out in the open, so Clay figured there was something down. He went over to see what it was. As he might have expected, it was a jackrabbit. There was no telling how it died, but it was laid out on its side with its left eye wide to the sky. There were a few tufts of fur on the grass, and as usual the magpie had started on the hind quarter, picking on the thigh meat and opening up the flank.

Clay was back to working on the firewood when he saw two riders approaching from the south. It looked like Sutton and Thode. He went into the shack and buckled on his gunbelt. Then he pulled out the .45, checked to see that it had five shells in the cylinder with the hammer on an empty chamber, and slid it back into the holster.

He took another look as he walked back toward the woodpile. It was Sutton and Thode, all right. He felt a knot tightening in his stomach as he picked up the ax. The feeling spread through him that these might be his last few minutes alive. He looked over to the east, a hundred yards away, where Rusty was picketed and grazing in the morning sun. That would be a bum way to go, with his firewood half chopped and his horse needing a drink.

Sutton and Thode rode up to him and faced him so that he had to look up at them into the sun.

'Good morning,' Clay said. He walked to the corner of his shack and leaned the ax against it, as he would have done to greet a welcome visitor. It gave him a better angle so he wasn't squinting into the sun. He was in front of Sutton and off to his right.

'I doubt it,' said Sutton, turning in the saddle and then holding his gray eyes on Clay as the big bay horse turned under him.

'Oh?' Clay got a good look at Sutton, and he felt a deep dislike for what he saw.

'I don't like squatters. Neither does my friend Mr Thode.'

'Did you ride over here this morning to tell me about your problems with your other neighbors?'

'I'm talkin' about you, Westbrook.'

Clay met him head on. 'If it's a matter of not liking me, you don't have to. If it's a matter of someone being a squter, I already explained to Mr Thode that I filed a homestead claim on this land and that he could go to the Land Office in Cheyenne if he had any doubts.'

'We did just that,' said Thode, who was on Sutton's left.

The left side of Thode's face was in shadow, but it looked cleared up. Clay thought he'd like to work on it again.

'And?'

'And I filed a claim on this very piece of land.' Thode wagged his head in the manner of saying 'I told you so.'

'How did you do that?'

'Call it influence,' Sutton snapped.

Clay looked back at Sutton. The blocky face was hard, with a trace of a smirk. Sutton looked very sure of himself. He must have bribed someone in the Land Office. . . . Or it could be a bluff. Sutton made a good stone wall. A man would never have guessed to look at him that he had offered Clay a job a month earlier.

Clay said, 'I've got papers.'

Thode said, 'I do, too.'

Sutton put his forearms on his saddle horn and leaned forward, continuing his mock politeness, as he said to Clay, 'Mr Thode and I try to get along with everyone.' Then he straightened up and put his hand on his thigh, in front of his holster and pistol. 'Even trespassers. Now I understand Mr Thode warned you once. Today we're warning you a second time. We won't warn you a third time.'

It seemed to Clay that Sutton was taking the lead even though it was supposedly Thode's claim. 'Did you come to do his talking for him? I thought maybe this would be between him and me.'

Thode jumped off his horse and came toward Clay, pulling off his gloves and stuffing them into his vest pocket. 'You damn right it is, you honyocker.'

Clay was squaring off. Thode was carrying a gun, but it looked like he wanted a fistfight. That was all right.

Sutton's voice stopped Thode. 'Get back on your horse, Alex.' Then he turned to Clay. 'I'm talking for both of us. Mr Thode is a touch shy, being new to the country. I don't like seeing his rights infringed on. He and I have a cooperative venture on this claim here, so it's an offense against my interests too. When it comes to negotiations, Mr Thode has confidence in my authority. And influence.'

Thode was back in the saddle, his face smoldering as he put on his gloves. The palomino sidestepped, and he slapped it on the neck with the loose ends of his reins.

Sutton spoke again. 'I'd say we've given you fair warning, Westbrook. Now you clear out, and that'll be the end of it.'

'And if I don't?'

'Then it won't.' Sutton reined his horse around and trotted off without looking back. It was obvious that he felt in control of the whole scene. Thode followed, but after a hundred yards his self-restraint must have worn thin, because he looked over his left shoulder and made a show of spitting.

Clay let his breath out. It was one thing after another, and Sutton wasn't letting up. It looked as if Clay was going to have to ride to Cheyenne. He wanted to take the borrowed ax and canvas back to Jackson Mead anyway, so he decided to get a levelheaded view on things before making a hasty trip. He put his own ax in the house, watered Rusty at the creek, and saddled up. Then, with the woodchopping still unfinished, he rode away.

Jackson Mead was untangling a hundred-foot rope when Clay rode up to the dugout. The two children, a boy and a girl aged five or six or so, were playing with a puppy while their mother sat in the sun in front of the dugout and mended one of Mead's buckskin shirts. She was a pretty woman, several years older than Lupita but still young looking. She smiled at Clay as she waved hello.

Mead explained that the snow would soon be melting in the mountains and he would be taking pilgrims up on pack trips. He was getting his gear ready. Clay helped him untangle the rope, which was a job a man liked to finish once he got started. Then they sat on the ground to talk.

When Clay had finished his story, Mead picked at the grass in front of him and said, 'They could be running a bluff. Or they could have pulled off a crooked piece of work that you may or may not be able to do anything about.'

'But I think I need to go to Cheyenne.'

'Probably so.'

'Today's Tuesday. If I leave in the morning, I can be back by Saturday in the evening. Travel light.'

Mead nodded. 'You might want to cache your plunder before you go, though.'

'How do you mean?'

'Well, I'd guess you've got a bed, and clothes, and a camp outfit, and some tools. I wouldn't just leave it all layin' there.'

'But it's my house.'

'If they're bluffin', it is, but that won't stop them from doin' what they want with your personal property. And if they aren't bluffin', you'll have to move it all anyway, at least until you get things straightened out.'

'That's true.'

'You can store it here, no problem. I doubt it's that much.'

'No. It's more than it was, but I bet I can get it on two horses.'

'Why don't we do that, then, and you won't have that to worry you while you're gone.'

Mead had three horses in a pole corral. He caught them one by one, putting a riding saddle on one and packsaddles on the other two. Then they headed for Clay's place.

'Nice-lookin' shack,' Mead said as they pulled up in front of it. 'It should last you a few years.'

'I hope so. Naturally, I'll want to build a real house later on.' Then Clay realized who he was talking to and said, 'You know.'

'Oh, yeah.'

It took about an hour to get Clay's belongings separated into equally weighted piles and then lashed on to the pack-saddles. Then each of the men took a lead rope and mounted up. As they were riding away, Clay looked back. It made him sad to be moving out so soon. It had been his home, and now, for the time being at least, it was just an eight-by-fifteen shack with a solid floor and an open doorway.

*

The next morning, Clay was up with the dawn and out on the trail. It was a pretty morning, with the meadowlarks on the ground and the hawks in the sky. Clay was glad he had taken Mead's advice and stored his belongings. He had enough to worry about with the Land Office, plus just making the trip. It was a four-day venture if he used his horse well. He pictured the entire loop, there and back. If anything went wrong, he wouldn't be able to see Lupita on Sunday. Naturally he could drop by anytime, but Sunday was her day off.

As he rode south, thinking more about Lupita, putting more distance between the two of them, his earlier feelings of uncertainty came back to him. He couldn't pinpoint exactly what it was that he felt unsure about – whether it was the idea of commitment to a woman once again, or whether it was the idea of this particular woman.

She had told him she didn't know him well – then it was probably true that he didn't know her well either. On one hand he felt as if he knew her in a deep and narrow way – that is, he had a basic, almost instinctive trust in her. But in other ways, he had to admit he barely knew her. She had her ways of language and customs and religion that he knew little about. She was dark and different from women he had known, and while he found her darkness appealing, even exciting, he also wondered if there was a basic difference that would eventually come between them. He knew that she was a person and he was a person, just as he and Rosalind had been, but he found himself wondering if they were different kinds of people. The possibility worried him, because he was afraid it might be true, even though he didn't want it to be.

The route he followed ran midway between and parallel to the two most frequently traveled roads north out of Cheyenne, so he had the country to himself. He figured he was on the eastern edge of the Silver Plains land, and by late morning he supposed he was close to the Courtland range.

That night he stayed at a ranch house south of Bear Creek. The custom of the country made travelers welcome at any ranch house. Distance and weather alone dictated the custom, and ranch people liked visitors who would bring news from up or down the trail and who would sit and visit for an evening. Clay passed the evening with a pleasant young couple who had taken up their homestead a few years earlier. They had two quarter sections and open land around theirs, and they were optimistic about the opportunities ahead of them. They had a little baby who cried all through supper, but the parents said he was cutting teeth and was usually an angel. These people were cheerful as they talked about natural calamities such as grasshoppers and hail. Their only real worry was sheep.

As for news, they said it was a bad year for coyotes. The husband said it had been a rough year for schoolteachers too, but he didn't get to elaborate. The wife, asking for news from up in Clay's territory and not getting any, said she had heard that the new rancher Sutton had a banker visiting and that they had had trouble with Mexicans. Clay wanted to say that Sutton was a thief and a liar, but instead he said that he didn't know of any Mexicans causing any trouble. Clay could tell that the husband wanted to tell the rest of the story about the schoolteacher, but the topic did not come around again.

On the second day, especially for the last ten miles on the way into Cheyenne, Clay's anxiety mounted. If Thode had filed successfully, Clay might end up walking away empty-handed or, worse in some ways, he could be stuck in Cheyenne indefinitely trying to straighten things out. One thing in his favor was that the weather was warm, so he slept in the hay in a livery stable and saved some money.

Clay was at the door of the U.S. Land Office when it opened at 9:00 A.M. A clerk about Clay's age, with mutton-chop whiskers and a prematurely balding head, looked up the case and shook his head.

'No problem at all, Mr Westbrook. You filed your claim on April 18, and you have five years to prove up on it.'

'No one else has filed on it or contested it?'

'Once you've filed on it, that action precludes another party from filing until you relinquish your claim. You won't receive a clear title until you've proven up, but you have your claim papers in the meanwhile.'

'And no one else has papers on that piece of land?'

The clerk shook his head solemnly, as if he were ages wiser than this fretful young cowpuncher. 'No, no one else could.'

Clay walked out into the morning sunlight. He could feel the anger pulsing in him. They had made a fool of him! Here he had ridden for two days, for nothing. Really, he thought, he should be happy, but he wasn't. He walked down the street, leading his horse and trying to calm down. Sutton and Thode would have to concede on this point. He could move back on to his land and see what improvements he could make next. One possibility under the provisions was to fence it. He winced at that thought, but it was an idea.

As he walked along the street, his attention was caught by a scene on his right. A wagon with a bed of straw was backed up through the open door of a warehouse. With the use of a rope, a pulley on a steel overhead track, and a huge pair of tongs, two men were hoisting a block of ice the size of a coffin.

Clay paused and looked at the ice as it hung in midair. Here it was June, bearing down on summer, and there was a block of ice. It must have been cut last winter, stored, shipped by rail, and now delivered to melt away far from its starting point.

It made him think of Sutton, whose father had been an ice merchant before the war, according to Highpockets. Clay thought about Sutton growing up with the residue of his father's Southern bitterness as the young man rubbed elbows with the buffalo hunters and bone scavengers. Now he cut the figure of a man of property, talking like a banker and lining up crews of men to claim land for him and dig big ditches. Clay shook his head. It was hard to imagine someone who had come that far and then wanted to rub out the common working folk whose stock he had come from. It was easier to understand Alex Thode.

Headed back north, Clay was on edge as much as he had been on the way to Cheyenne. Now he was incensed at Sutton and Thode for sending him on this chase, he was impatient to get back and reclaim his property, and he was anxious to visit Lupita again. He was keyed up enough to ride straight through, but to treat his horse decently, he camped on Bear Creek. He was in the vicinity of the couple he had stayed with, and they had invited him to stop over on his way back, but he was too churned up to spend an evening with his feet underneath someone's kitchen table.

Clay slept on the ground in his clothes, using his slicker as a ground sheet and the saddle blanket as a quilt. When he opened his eyes in the gray of morning he saw a dark shape on the opposite creek bank. At first he thought it might be a wild turkey. He felt for his pistol beside him. Then he saw that it was a hawk, a large one, sitting on a dead rabbit. The hawk had a method. He would dip his sharp beak into the rabbit and come up with a strip of food. He would look to each side as he swallowed the grub, and then he would go down for another dip. It was a fierce pattern, ripping up a bite and then looking both ways to see if there was any danger. Sometimes the strip he came up with looked like a loop of intestine; at other times it looked like a shred of flesh. Tufts of fur lay scattered around like feathers. Clay remembered times when he was cleaning a rabbit and there was no water at hand. Bits of fur would cling to the meat and end up singed on to it when it was cooked. The fur never seemed to bother animals, but of course they took their meat raw. Clay was still for a long time, not wanting to disturb the bird.

He closed his eyes. Soon he was asleep. He dreamed about a man who looked quite a bit like Sutton, hard-faced and beefy, and he had his arm around a woman who looked like Rosalind. The man was smirking as he talked, and a shine spread over his face. Clay tried to hit him but couldn't reach him. Then he got his hands on him, held the shirt and jacket with his left hand, and smashed him with his right. The woman wasn't there anymore, and Clay punched the man solidly time and again. He was elated, feeling refreshed and lighter. He woke up and saw that the hawk was still working on his meal, so Clay closed his eyes again.

Clay still didn't move. He didn't want to make the bird flap away, and he wanted to think about the dream. It was a short dream but vivid. He felt justified in clobbering his enemy, and it made him feel good. It had been quite a release. He thought about the man he had envisioned. It was some combination of Sutton and Murdock.

Clay lay very still, working on the idea. He just wanted to get even, that was all. He hadn't wanted to kill anyone since he was up in the Missouri breaks. He wanted to punish Murdock, but he was powerless to do it. Now Murdock was twisted up with Sutton, had been since the first day on the river. It made sense. They were the same – a liar, a thief, an opportunist with women. Of late it all took shape in the form of Sutton and Thode, and mostly Sutton. Thode was a side matter, a proud little rooster who had knocked off Clay's hat. Sutton was the bugbear, looming over Clay. He could take Sutton down to size in his own mind if he could untangle him from Murdock.

Clay must have shifted beneath the skimpy blanket, for the hawk flapped up and away. Clay rolled out and got up and moving. As he took his horse to water, he felt cool and clear inside. He had his enemies sorted out and he knew them apart.

It was still a full day's ride if he didn't push the horse and if he took the wide way around the Silver Plains range. In the afternoon he saw thunderclouds off to the west in the direction of his own place, and he hoped his grass would catch some of the rain.

He made it to Jackson Mead's place by early Saturday evening, as planned. Mead said he had been to town that afternoon and had heard nothing. He offered Clay a fresh horse to ride out and check on his place. Clay decided to do that before taking his bedroll down from the rafter pole of Mead's stable. These were the longest days of the year, so he would have time to take a look.

The sky was clear now, and the air was fresh. Clay could smell wet grass and wet earth. Then, as he got closer to his homestead, he caught a smell that meant danger and stirred fear on the prairie. The smell was wet now, but he knew what it meant. He knew what he would see before he saw it, but the sight still made him run cold. There ahead of him on the prairie, where his shack had been, was a black scab of rubble and ashes. The sons of bitches had even burned his firewood – and he knew who they were.

CHAPTER 11

Jackson Mead shook his head as he heard Clay's story. Although he had admired Clay's shack while it was standing, he didn't seem to think that its being burned was a loss of great value. He was more disgusted by the act itself. 'You'd think they would've let it look like lightning, at least, but they tossed on all the firewood too?'

'Yeah. And they didn't let the fire spread. The grass is green, but there was good dry stuff from the winter, and none of it got burned.'

'It might have if it had just been Thode. But Sutton knows the country.'

'Probably wanted to save the grass for his own stock.'

'That, too.'

As Clay rolled out his bed that night in the stable, he was glad he had taken Mead's advice and saved his belongings. He was burned out, but he wasn't entirely wiped out.

The next morning, as he sat in the sunlight drinking coffee with Jackson Mead, Clay brought up the topic of his interest in Lupita Fuentes. He hadn't had the chance to speak to anybody about it, and he felt he wanted to. If there was anyone he knew who would understand and whose judgment he could trust in this matter, it would be Mead. The older man listened and smiled as Clay told about meeting her and being attracted to her. Clay was glad to talk about things he had kept so much to himself. His story seemed real and normal as he told it, thanks in part to the encouragement he was getting from Mead.

He hesitated when he came to the part about color, the question about difference, but he knew it was a part he had to bring up. So he did.

'There's one thing I don't know what to think of,' he said.

'And what's that?'

'Well, it's her – darkness.'

Mead raised his eyebrows as if to say, 'Go ahead.'

'She's got beautiful hair and beautiful skin. I'm really taken by it, you know? But I'm wondering if it should be telling me something.'

'Like what?'

'Well, like maybe we're different, too different, and I'm just trying not to see it.'

Mead shook his head.

'No?'

'Not at all. It's not like oil and water. You're a man and she's a woman. Any other differences between you are the same kind you'd have between you and someone just as white as you are. Or whiter.'

Clay laughed. It was a relief to hear it put that way. 'I thought you'd be a good person to ask,' he said.

It was Mead's turn to laugh. 'I'm no expert,' he said, 'but I did have a lily-white little wife at one time, for whever that's worth. We didn't have much understanding between us. This woman I have now, she and I do. That's the difference. If you and this girl have an understanding, that's all you need.' Mead paused and cocked his head. 'Well, it's not everything, I'll admit that.'

They both laughed. Then Clay said, 'How about these other things, like language and religion and how they do things?'

Mead pushed out his lower lip and nodded. Then he said, 'Those are important, for damn sure. But that's part of what you need to have your understanding about, both ways. It doesn't have to be a problem. It can make everything a lot more interesting. As far as language goes, you say she speaks perfect English. That's better than my wife and I do, but we don't have any trouble getting the ideas out.'

Clay nodded. 'Sounds like everything's all right. In my case, I mean.'

'Uh-huh. Then whatever was eatin' on you wasn't the color itself.'

'No, I just thought maybe there was something I wasn't letting myself see. Some reason why this might not be a good idea.'

'Oh, there could be, with some people. But I think that comes from the color itself. There's some white people that don't see a dark person as a person. They look on 'em like they're some kind of animal. They look at my wife that way. Makes me want to kill 'em for a moment or two, but I know I can't change it. Anyway, you're not that way. I know that much.'

'No.'

'Well, let me put it to you this way.' Mead looked him in the eyes. 'What do you think of havin' kids who are a mix?'

'That would be fine, especially if they look like her.'

'Then I don't think you have a problem. Not in that area, anyway. But you want to make sure you understand each other.

And then you've still got the rest of the world to deal with.'

Clay nodded. He understood the last comment to include his problems with Sutton and Thode, as well as whatever attitudes might come his way about mixed marriage, if he went that far. He plucked at the grass in front of him where he sat. He looked at Mead and smiled, and the older man just smiled and nodded back.

From that point the conversation went on and changed course. They got around to the topic of where Clay was to live.

Clay said he had decided to camp north of the river, near town. The night before, Mead had invited him to camp there on Stone Creek. Clay gave his reasoning for camping elsewhere. 'If I can find some work in town, maybe I can get a stake together and rebuild. I've got to get back on to that place and do something to hold it.' The other part of it, which he thought would have sounded silly if he'd said it out loud, was that he wanted to put the river between him and Sutton for the time being.

Mead listened and agreed. 'You can build another shack,' he said, 'when you get around to it.'

Clay went on to say that he wondered if he could buy a tent on credit. He hadn't minded the canvas shelter he had rigged up before, he said, but he would like something that was better at keeping out the weather.

'We might work up a trade,' said Mead.

Clay looked at him. Mead had trapped and traveled enough among the Indians and the whites that he was naturally a trader. He had been quick to help Clay look out for his portable property. Out of habit, he saw the value of anything that could be traded and put on a horse's back. Things had value measured against one another and not just in terms of whispering cash. Clay had known him to value this knife at three fox furs, that horse at a lever-action rifle, and so forth. If he had a trade, it would be a fair one.

'Let's hear it,' Clay said.

'You have a set of tools that you don't need right now and can't rightly pack around with you, or don't need to. And I have a camp tent that's just about what you need.'

Clay was surprised. 'Do you think you need those tools?'

'Not at all. But I can hold on to 'em. If you want to trade back for 'em later, we can do that, and if not, I can trade 'em easy enough. It's money in the bank to me.'

'You won't be out of a tent now, will you?'

'Oh, no. I've got another one.'

Clay thought it over, weighing the tools against a tent he hadn't seen. 'I'll want to keep my ax,' he said, 'so I won't have to turn around and borrow one from you. The rest of it I think I can do without.'

'Well, mister,' said Mead in a fair imitation of a Southern accent, 'you got yerself a tent.'

Clay used the ax to cut tent poles and stakes. By midafternoon he had the tent set up and pegged down. For his campsite he chose a spot upstream from the base of the bluff that overlooked the twin rivers. It was also close to the spot where he had had his first trouble with Sutton and Thode, but he brushed aside that detail as he thought of his last visit to the bluff. With his bedroll, clothes, and camp gear stowed inside the tent, he thought he had enough time to clean up and pay a visit. After a wash at the river he put on his cleanest shirt, tied the tent flap closed, and rode to Mexican town.

It was well after the dinner hour as Clay took the lane off the main road and into the layout of houses. He smiled to himself. He wouldn't mind a good feed right now, but it was just as well he didn't show up each time as the tortillas were stacking up.

It was a joke in ranch country. If company showed up just at dinner, someone was likely to make a remark about whipping the horses to get there in time. Clay was sure that the Campos family was always happy to have him share their food, and he was too, but today he thought it was all right to be breaking the pattern.

Tony wasn't at home. He had gone to the stockyards to check on the cattle. The women immediately got it out of Clay that he hadn't eaten, and before he knew it he was dipping tortilla pieces into a plate of refried beans.

Lupita sat at the table as Clay put away his meal. With these people, he never felt self-conscious about eating. It was very comfortable, and far more graceful than wolfing a plate of grub at the campfire. Today, all that was left from the midday meal was beans, but Clay was happy to eat and Margarita was happy to dish him up.

He did not overlook Lupita, however. His pulse had quickened as soon as he saw her, and he knew his feelings about her were right. She had given him her hand when he first came in, and the warm touch stayed with him even as he sat across the table. She was wearing a white dress, a lightweight dress that seemed to go with the warming weather. Clay could see more of her throat than he had seen before, and he also saw a delicate gold chain that held a crucifix. As always, he was moved by the sight of her long dark hair, wavy and shiny against the smooth brown texture of her cheek and neck.

'Did you miss me?' he asked, hoping she would see the tease.

'Well, yes,' she answered, smiling and then looking down for an instant. Then she looked up and said, 'My uncle said not to worry, you were probably busy. When you didn't come today, we thought maybe you were still busy.'

'Well, I've been busy,' he said, 'but I've missed you.'

'Thank you,' she said, looking down. The long eye-lashes went down and then up.

Clay took a quick deep breath. It was a feeling such as he might have at the edge of a pool of water – a deep, clear pool.

She looked up, and her face was bright as she smiled. Her eyes sparkled.

He needed to make some small talk. 'Have things been going all right at work?'

'Oh, yes,' she said. 'And you?'

He phrased his answer carefully. 'I was working on my place until yesterday. Now I think I'll look for work here in town.'

'That's good. Maybe you can work with my uncle.'

'I'll see what comes up.'

'Would you like more to eat?'

'No, thank you. I had two helpings. That means I liked it, you know.'

She smiled. 'I know.'

She asked him if he would like some coffee, and he said yes. She took his plate to the kitchen, where he heard her talking to Margarita. In a little while she came back with a cup of tan coffee and set it in front of him. Then she returned to the kitchen and came back with the sugar.

'Do you like the coffee that way?'

'I'm learning to.'

'How do you usually drink coffee?'

'Black. That's the way they all make it out there. Sometimes a fellow will take sugar.' He looked at her as he took a spoonful.

She made a small smile and looked happy. 'We call it *café con leche.*'

'Again?'

'*Café con leche,*' she said, with crisp, rounded sounds.

'Coffay cone lechay,' he repeated.

'Close,' she said, smiling broadly. 'We'll teach you.'

'I'll learn.' He stirred his coffee and sipped it. 'It's good. I like it.'

'Good.'

He paused, wondering what to say next. They'd talked about work and food. He couldn't bring himself to go right into the weather for his next topic. Then it occurred to him to ask about church.

'Did you go to church today?'

'Well, yes. We go to church, um, frequently. But we didn't have mass today. We had it last week, and then again next week.'

'Oh, I see.'

She seemed to hesitate as she asked him, 'Do you have a church?'

Clay widened his eyebrows. 'Well, no, not really. I haven't been to churches much since I left home – in fact, not at all – and it wasn't a real big habit of mine before that.'

She was quiet.

Then he saw daylight. 'That doesn't mean I don't like church or that I'm opposed to it. It just means that I'm pretty – uh, open, I guess.'

A half-smile played on her face.

Clay heard a chorus of laughter from in back of the house, where the boys were usually running around before and after dinner. He motioned with his head toward the back and asked, 'How are the boys?'

'They're fine. Marcos really liked your horse.'

That was where he wanted to be in the conversation. 'We ought to see about giving him another ride.'

She looked at him with the half-smile.

'What would you think about going for a walk again?'

'To the same place?'

'If you'd like.'

'Yes, I would like that. It was very pretty up there.'

'Do you think you can force Marcos to go along?'

She laughed. 'I think so. I'll go ask my aunt.'

Clay heard a short exchange in the kitchen, and then he heard Margarita go to the back door. She called out the boy's name in two long syllables, and then in a voice not so loud she said something that sounded like a full sentence and ended with *¡ándale!*

Marcos came through the kitchen grinning and walked over to shake Clay's hand. Clay stood up and shook the boy's hand, asked him if he was ready to ride the horse, then picked up his hat. Lupita came back into the room wearing a gray shawl, and they were ready to go.

It was a warm day, verging on being hot. They strolled along with the chaperone riding silently in back of them. By the time they got to the top of the bluff, Lupita was perspiring lightly. They stood on the top, where there was a faint breeze. She used the shawl to pat the dampness on her forehead. Clay liked it. He liked a woman who wasn't afraid to sweat a little, especially when she looked so pretty patting it away.

'Hot?' he asked.

'Just a little,' she said.

'It can get hotter here.' Then he remembered where she worked and he said, 'But I guess you know what's hot and what isn't. This is probably cool compared to the bakery.'

She nodded, shaking the shawl so that it lay loosely across the back of her shoulders. 'This is nice here,' she said. 'It's free and clean, and peaceful.' She looked away to the southwest and said, 'Your land is over there?'

'Yep.'

'And you live there?'

'I did. You see, I built a little house there, just for myself. I was out there for a couple of weeks.'

'Wasn't it lonely?'

Clay would have liked to hear more romance in the question,

but it was asked in the same tone as when she said he must miss his family. 'I kept pretty busy,' he said, 'but I did get lonely. I had plenty of time to think.'

'And now you don't live in the house?'

'Well, no, I can't, because somebody burned it down.' He heard her breathe in sharply. 'Someone doesn't like me for a neighbor,' he went on, 'and burned me out.'

She looked at him with her eyebrows drawn.

'I've got a pretty good hunch that it was these same two big wheels. They came along and tried to run me off, and then when I was gone for a while, they put a match to it. I assume they did it. The only good thing was that I'd got my belongings out first.' He pointed at his tent down on the grassy swale, nearly a half mile away. 'That's where I've got my camp now.'

She looked at it, opening her eyes. 'A tent.'

'Good enough for now,' he said.

They stood for a long moment in the warm sunlight. Then she said, 'And this is the only real trouble you've had?'

'Well, there was that other bad spell I went through before, that I told you about.'

'Was it like this?'

'No, it was nothing like it. Well, I guess it was like it in some ways. But no, that other fella didn't come around to torment me. He went away and stayed away.'

'Oh.'

Clay had noticed that Lupita usually stopped short of making a personal question. She either asked it broadly or let him take the lead, as she did now. So he went ahead and gave her a short account of how another man had stolen his girl, going light on the part about his supposed roll in the hay.

'And you didn't do anything to get in trouble?'

Clay imagined a good old-fashioned knife in the ribs, and he laughed. 'No. It just made me sick, like I said the other day.'

She gave him a questioning look.

'I hated him so much for what he did to me, it was like poison in my blood. And I can't say it's all gone yet.'

'It was her fault, too.'

Clay turned. This was as direct as he'd known her to be.

Moreover, hearing it said out loud had a surprising effect on him. He hadn't thought of it in such strong terms. 'In what way?' he asked, not disagreeing as much as hoping to see one woman's point of view about another woman.

'She should have waited. She didn't know what happened to you. She should have waited until you came back.' Lupita gave him an earnest look.

'But he lied to her.'

'She should have known he was a liar.' She shook her head very slightly.

'Would you?'

'Oh, yes, I know a liar.'

'No, I mean, would you wait?'

'Of course.'

'Maybe it was more her fault than I give her credit for.' In that moment, it washed over him that he had been obsessed with blaming Murdock so he wouldn't have to blame Rosalind. He went on, 'I hated him so much, that's all I wanted to see. And I carried it around with me like a carpetbag.'

She put her hand on his arm. 'It's in the past, Clay.'

Their eyes met and he thought he could kiss her right there, except that forty yards away, Marcos was riding Rusty in a lazy circle. All the chaperone had to do was be there.

'I'm going to try to see it that way,' he said, 'instead of staying worked up about what went on and why it happened.'

'Maybe God wanted it.'

Clay remembered the knot in his stomach that he had carried for so long. 'Why would he want that?'

Her hand was still on his arm, and he felt it there as she said, 'We don't know. Maybe it was so we could meet each other.'

Their eyes met again, and her left hand slid down his forearm as his right hand raised to meet it. The warmth of their hands pressing together sent a surge through him. He took a deep breath and then said, 'I'm glad we met.'

'So am I,' she said.

'I wasn't sure if you were. I didn't know if you wanted to go out for a walk the first time I asked you. But I knew I'd be mad at myself if I didn't ask.'

'You did the right thing,' she said, nodding. 'The man is supposed to take the initiative.'

'And what if you wouldn't have wanted to?'

'Then you wouldn't have asked.' She smiled.

That was part of the code, Clay thought – the part about his having to take the initiative. It went along with the business about the stern father figure who had to keep a wall between himself and the young man. That was all right. If he wanted to live in her world and wanted her to live in his, he had better be willing to accept her codes. That was plumb fine. He didn't have any interest in being boss anyway.

Her hand was still in his as he looked at the river. He looked down at her hand, dark against his. He knew he was falling in love with her, not despite her darkness and not because of it. The idea that had troubled him on the road to Cheyenne was not a worry now, but he was glad to have talked it through. The conversation with Jackson Mead had helped him clear his mind. The moment of truth had been when he first saw her today, and again now, as he saw their hands together.

He looked around at Marcos, who was singing a soft low song in Spanish and riding the horse in a wandering circle. Then Clay looked back at the river, at the glistening current that was one, and two, and one again. He felt a boldness flow through him as he heard himself say, 'It's like magic, isn't it?'

Her hand was warm and steady as she gazed at the river and answered, 'Yes. It's just like us.'

CHAPTER 12

Clay awoke to the chattering of magpies. He could picture the gang of them in the dead cottonwood on the cut-bank. The sound of the birds came right through the tent wall, as did the rushing sound of the river. From the other side came the shift and plod of hoofs and the crunching and tearing of grass as Rusty grazed.

Maybe it was a magpie morning instead of a meadowlark morning, but Clay felt the world was quite a bit better place than it had been the morning before, when he woke up with the smell of burned lumber and tarpaper in his nostrils. He thought of the conversation he and Lupita had had the day before, and it all made sense. Her hand in his made the most sense of all, but the other parts of the conversation had brought him even further along in getting his mind settled about Murdock and Rosalind. He could let them both go. He saw that he had clung to Rosalind because he thought they should still be in love, and he had clung to Murdock so he could blame him for everything. Now, by admitting that Rosalind could come in for some of the blame, he could let go of that whole ordeal. Along with it might go the resistance he had felt toward committing himself to a woman once again. To put the idea into Lupita's words, he could leave it all in the past.

That left Sutton – Sutton and Thode – to deal with. There was a problem that wasn't in the past, not as of the day before yesterday. They had burned him out and probably thought they had run him off his property, but they didn't have claim to the land and they still had a personal grudge against him. They wouldn't let up yet. He was sure he would have more business with them. He wouldn't have to go looking for it, but he was going to have to see it through.

Outside the tent, Clay saw that it was going to be overcast. The sun was coming up, but it didn't look like it was going to break through. That was the way the weather was this time of year – fluctuating. A good part of the time, a storm would build up in the afternoon, let go, and clear out. Most of the day would be sunny and pleasant, an hour or so would make a fellow glad he owned a slicker, and then the evening would be clean and clear with birds chirping till sundown. At other times, like now, a mass of clouds could move in and hang over the area for a few days. It might drizzle off and on, or it might just hang overhead like a wet layer of gray felt. Things didn't dry out well then. Trails were slick, bedrolls were damp. It looked like he was in for a spell of that kind of weather, and he was glad he had the tent.

Clay built a fire and stood by it. As soon as it burned down a little bit, he would set the coffeepot in closer and get it going. He looked across the fire at the river and saw what he had noticed when he was gathering firewood. The river was rising. With the summer rains and the snowmelt higher up, the river would be at flood stage in many places. It was safer here, where there was higher ground on both sides. Clay looked at the ground around him and thought he had his camp in a pretty good place.

He looked back at the river. A swollen river was a cowboy's nightmare. Those who brought the trail herds north had a thousand campfire stories about the river crossings. Cattle, good horses, and good men had all gone under. It was a fear that was shared by cowboys, whether it was formed firsthand or was passed by word of mouth, or, as it sometimes seemed, was something they were born with. Many of the cowpunchers Clay had met didn't know how to swim. Even a person like himself, who could swim all right, would have a rough go if his boots filled up and his clothes got soaked. Men told stories about how they tied their boots and clothes on top of the saddle and, wearing their hat and underwear, they grabbed the horse's tail and made it across.

Those stories were rarely humorous. They had graduated into campfire stories because something memorable had happened, and often the memorable part was summed up in the short phrase, 'and we buried him there.' Clay put his hands to the fire. There were plenty of ways to die, and few people welcomed any of them; but nobody wanted to drown. He had even heard one man say, 'That was how I got here. I don't want to go back that way.'

Clay thought of the old song 'Bury Me Not on the Lone Prairie.' More than a few cowpunchers disliked the song. They said they were tired of it, that it had been sung too much. Maybe it had. In some outfits it was a rule that you couldn't sing it if anyone was around to hear it. But more than being worn out, which a lot of songs were, it was a haunting song. Anyone who had lived and worked on the lone prairie, and had heard that song, had to wonder if he would be buried there.

The fire burned down to coals and a hot flame. Clay set the coffee pot on a V of two flat rocks that jutted into the coals. He rummaged in the tent and found the last of his raisins, which would be the other half of breakfast. Grub was getting low again, and he needed to go to town to see about work, anyway. The thought made him queasy. Anyone who knew him would know he had been fired, or at least he would feel that way when people looked at him.

With his jackknife he punched two small holes in an air-tight can of milk. He had gotten to like *café con leche* at Tony's house, and he thought he'd try his own version. Condensed milk was stronger than fresh milk, so he wouldn't need much. He poured a cup of coffee and then tipped in a stream of the cream-colored milk. He broke a matchstick, plugged the two holes, and set the can aside. Then he sipped the coffee. It wasn't as good, but it reminded him of her, even without the sugar.

After breakfast, being in no hurry to go to town, he decided to bring in a supply of firewood before it rained. He didn't have a way to keep it out of the rain, since his saddle and other belongings took up just about all the floor space inside the tent, but he could stack it so that quite a bit of it would stay dry. If he put the thicker pieces on top, he could split them to get a dry surface to burn. Then recalling what had happened to his last heap of firewood, he shook his head. He couldn't let that stop him. He had to start over and hope his work wouldn't be undone again.

As he moved his clothes to uncover the ax where he had left it the day before, he saw his rifle. It would be good to have a deer, he thought, but it wasn't good weather for hanging one. He pulled a winter coat back over the rifle and went out with the ax.

Chopping wood was good exercise. It made him feel clean inside. Maybe it was helping him get rid of the poison. It made him feel strong and capable – capable of protecting and providing. It also gave him the feeling that he was getting somewhere again. Every length of firewood added to the stack.

He rested, holding the end of the ax handle upright next to his leg. They could take his job or burn him to the ground, kick him from one place to another, but he was going to come right back at it. He would get by. Give him an ax and a rifle, and a bucket, and he could make do for the two of them. He smiled, raised his eyebrows, and went back to chopping.

Later that day, he went to town. Clay wasn't overly fond of

towns to begin with, and under the present circumstances he didn't like going from place to place and asking people if they knew of any work. It was discouraging as he went through it. The answer was the same in every place he went, and he didn't take it personally.

'Things are pretty slow right now. Everyone's out on roundup.' That was what he heard up and down Main Street. The railroad had already come through, the big ditch hadn't started yet, and nesters didn't hire anyone. Most of the hiring was for ranch work. At another time of the year he might have heard, 'Things are pretty slow right now. Wait till roundup.' Or in the fall, 'Things are slowed down now, with roundup over and the cattle all shipped.' He imagined that people on Main Street were repeating to him what they said day in and day out to one another. Things were probably slow most of the time – only the reasons changed.

The best places for finding out about work were saloons and barbershops. The cowpuncher Slim had successfully migrated from one to another, and he had a job. Two-Dollar Bill always declared that the best place to find a job was in a saloon. Then he might add, with a grin, that it was a damn good place to lose one, too. At any rate, a saloon was a place where men congregated to hear news, spread news, look for work, look for help, read a newspaper, or wait out the rain. It was especially so in the daytime and in a town such as this one, which did not yet have a hotel with a lobby. Barbershops were good places too, but they did not attract such a variety and they did not have as many chairs for loiterers. Although Clay didn't have any money to throw around, he felt better as a paying customer, so he got a haircut and then went to the Red Rose and drank a beer. On his way out, he saw the bakery up the street. He nodded in that direction, then unhitched his horse, swung on, and rode out of town.

The trip to town had managed to take up most of the afternoon. By the time Clay had his new supply of grub put away, he figured it was past five o'clock. The sun still hadn't come out. He thought that in good weather he would like to be on top of the bluff to see the sunset. Today, though, it probably wouldn't matter. It would be a good four hours till sunset, and the sky wasn't likely to clear even by then.

Clay had left his name around town, along with where he was staying, so he knew he would be easy to find. He was not surprised, then, when about an hour later he saw Alex Thode riding his way. The surprise was that Thode was by himself. He must have been in town and couldn't resist the temptation to pass this way on his trip back. Clay went into the tent and came back out wearing his gunbelt. He smiled to himself as he thought, *Try to get the sun at your back today.*

Thode brought his horse to a stop just short of Clay's firepit and woodpile, a few yards from the entrance of the tent. The palomino lifted its tail and dropped a few road apples. Clay thought, what a little pig. Doesn't even know he should stop his horse a ways out, give it a breather, and let it relieve itself there. Sutton would know that. If he hadn't learned it early on, the buffalo hunters would have slapped it into him.

'Well, look who's here,' said Thode, as if he hadn't expected to see the man he saw.

'Fancy that,' Clay answered. He noticed Thode wasn't wearing his gloves.

'Is this your summer home?'

'This is it, period. You know damn well I got burned out.'

'What do you mean?'

'You know what I mean. *Someone* set fire to my shack when I was down in Cheyenne.'

'The hell you say.'

'The hell I do say. I rode all the way to Cheyenne, and I found out nobody's touched my claim. It's clear and free.'

Thode raised his eyebrows. 'I'm surprised Mr Sutton made a mistake like that. I must have the claim next to it, then.'

'I bet. You can play dumb all you want, but I'll tell you, it didn't do any good to burn my shack. The land's still mine, and I'll be back.'

'You should be careful about what you say, boy. Don't just tell a man you think he burned down your house.'

Clay could tell that Thode had borrowed some of Sutton's manner and was trying to be a gentleman cowboy. 'Why don't you cut out the act?' he said. 'It's plain as day what happened. You and Sutton try to run me off, and then the place goes up in smoke.'

'Are you sure you didn't go off and leave a fire burning?' Thode raised his eyebrows.

'Don't try to feed me that. Someone burned my house and tossed the firewood in to boot. And you know it.'

'To tell you the truth, I didn't know it. I thought you were still there, gettin' ready to plant spuds.'

Clay could feel himself building up. It was what Thode wanted, he could tell, but he wasn't going to play into it.

'That's why I was surprised to see you here,' Thode went on.

'I bet.'

'When I rode up, I thought maybe you'd come to town to get a haircut.'

'Uh-huh.'

'Then I thought maybe you'd made your camp here so you could be closer to your little chili-choker.'

That did it. Clay could feel his face and ears burning, and he heard himself say, 'Get off your horse, Thode, or go home like the tinhorn coward you are.'

'My pleasure,' said Thode, and he swung down from the saddle. He took off his gunbelt and hooked it on his saddle horn, then put his clean white hat over that.

He must have seen a cowboy do that, Clay thought, as he dropped his own hat and gunbelt inside the tent.

Thode had his dukes up and was ready to go, as if he had taken boxing lessons. His left fist was above his right fist, in front of his chin, and both elbows were straight down. Clay put up his fists in his own way, at chest height. Both fighters circled to the right, and the palomino backed away.

When Clay had his back to the firewood and pit, Thode came at him. Clay stood his ground and took one on the right cheekbone, but Thode walked into a solid counter-punching left hook. They separated and circled again.

Clay faked a step forward and drew a punch, a left jab that grazed him on the right cheek. That was what he thought. Thode's style was to lunge, left foot and left jab. A right cross was sure to follow. That was fine. Thode had probably never fought with bare fists and didn't realize that he had less to block and less to block with.

Clay drew another lunge, took two to the face, and then caught Thode with a good left hook. Thode dropped his guard and then Clay stepped into him with a right and a left. Thode went back against the woodpile and scattered it.

He was back on his feet then, bouncing and circling until he apparently decided on a new tactic. He settled into a more closed stance, leading with his left leg and left elbow, hunching over and making small circles with his left fist.

That style came from another lesson, Clay thought. Then the left fist came flicking at him, and he stepped aside. Thode planted his left boot and came up with his right boot. It was anybody's rules.

Clay dropped his left hand and turned aside, and then, cupping the raised boot just above the heel, he yanked Thode around. Thode's left foot came right up from under him, and his butt dropped hard to the ground.

Thode's face was twisted in pain as he brought his left elbow up and around in front of him where he was sitting. Clay thought about kicking him in the face or busting him a few more in the chops as he came back up, but he held back. He had gotten in a few good punches, and if Thode came back for more, he'd see about giving it to him.

Thode just sat there, holding his left elbow with his right hand. He was out of the fight and obviously wasn't expecting any more.

'Had enough?'

Thode wouldn't look up or say anything. He just rolled to one side and got up, keeping his back to Clay, and walked to his horse. He put his hat on his head and then, with obvious pain, buckled on his gunbelt. He pulled the gloves out of his right vest pocket and put them on. Then, still with his back to Clay and the camp, he pushed the horse around, pulled himself aboard, and rode back toward town.

Clay was still wound up and ready to go, but the fight was long over. He watched Thode dip out of sight, and then he went to restack his firewood. It was too bad, he thought. It would have been good to thrash him a little more, or make him square up about the claim filing and the torch job. Maybe make him eat his words about Lupita. That was the way things went, though. He didn't get to make Thode admit or take back anything, and all he had was the satisfaction of getting in a few good punches. Furthermore, he might have just made things worse.

CHAPTER 13

Clay awoke to the magpies again. It had drizzled during the night, but as he looked around inside the tent it didn't look like any water had gotten in. He thought he had pitched the tent on a good swell of ground, and so far it all looked fine. If he got a steady rain for a length of time he might wish he had a tarpaper shack or a cot in a bunkhouse, but wishing wouldn't change anything. This was where he was until he worked back into something better.

As he rolled out of bed, he could feel the spots where he had taken the punches the day before. Thode had to be feeling quite a bit worse. Clay wondered who had been pushed around more at this point, himself or Thode. It certainly wasn't Sutton.

Clay checked on his horse and then got a fire going. The magpies were gone, and there didn't seem to be another creature around except for him and the horse. He thought of the boys out on roundup, the herd of workhorses, and the crowding bunches of cattle. Even here, close to town, things could get lonely. The gloomy weather helped it seem that way. He looked at the sky. It was likely to rain some more.

He took the bucket down to the river and poked it in, dipping it with the current, the low side of the rim downstream to get less trash. The river was running high, and there was quite a bit of debris on the surface. He pulled the bucket up dripping and carried it back to the campsite. The water could settle while the fire burned down. He could skim it and then pour the cleanest water from the top. Then it would boil in the coffeepot, and it would be all right.

The smell of coffee and bacon cheered things up. He rolled a log dry side up and sat down. The hot grub went well with the cold biscuits from the day before. He was pouring a second cup of coffee when the rustle of raindrops on cottonwood leaves added to the gurgle of the river. He set the plate next to the frying pan on the ground, grabbed the coffeepot and cup, and went into the tent.

The rain came down. It drummed on the tent canvas, thudded on the ground outside. He looked out through the tent flap, and all he could see was sheets of rain. It made him feel closed off from the rest of the world, an island, with nothing but the gray elements stretching away on all sides.

Finally the rain let up, although the sky didn't clear. It wasn't good weather to ride anywhere, but at least he could go out and stretch his legs.

It was a long day with nothing to do. It would be a good day to play cards or take a bath, even read one of Jamie's books. All he could do was piddle around camp.

Around six o'clock, Tony Campos came riding up on his mouse-colored horse. He was wearing a canvas overcoat and a narrow-brimmed gray felt hat, and he looked like he had something bothering him.

'The sonofabitches,' he said, before he even got off his horse.

'What did they do?'

'The sonofabitches,' he repeated, sliding off the horse with his hand on the cantle.

'What happened?'

'They kilt my sheep.'

'All of them?'

'No, just young ones. Lambs.'

'Where were they when they did it?'

'In the corral. The sheep pen.'

'Just now? Today?'

'No, last night. It musta been last night when it was dark, the middle of the night.'

'And you just found out about it?'

'My boys take care of the sheep in the morning, and I was at work all day. My wife, she's all nervous. She's been worryin' all day.'

'I don't blame her.'

'Clay, it's gotta be those same two big shots, huh?'

'Well, that's what I'd think right off. Let's go through it again. Someone got into your sheep pen in the middle of the night and killed all your lambs.'

'Not all of 'em. Six. I still got five.'

'All right. They killed six lambs. Did they shoot them? Did anybody hear any shots?'

'No, they musta hit 'em all in the head. That's what it look like. You know, some of 'em have blood comin' outa the nose, or the ears. None of 'em got the throat cut, or no bullet holes.'

'Just hit 'em with a club?'

'Yeah, I think so. That's what it look like.'

'Well, I don't think it was Thode. He came by here at about this time yesterday, or a little earlier, and he and I had it out. He left nursing his elbow, and I don't think he was up to even climbing a fence, much less clubbing sheep.'

'What do you think about the other one?'

'Sutton? I'd bet he was behind it, but he was probably miles away, with someone to vouch for him.'

'So he paid someone, probably.'

'That would be my guess. No way to prove it. It's like the way they burned my shack. I guess Lupita told you about that.'

'Yeah. She said you built a little house, and they burnt it.'

'I guess it was them, just like I suppose they had your sheep killed. It's a low-down way to do things, but that's what we're up against.' As he spoke, Clay realized that this attack on Tony carried a message for him.

'Can't do nothin'. That's the bad part.' Tony shook his head.

'I don't know what they can do next. If they wanted to kill us, I think they would have done it by now.'

'They can kill more sheep.'

'Yes, they can do that. But they probably feel they made their point. They could have killed more while they were at it.'

'Yeah, they know I'll be waitin' for 'em. And I will be.' Tony flashed his white smile for the first time.

Clay laughed lightly. Then he said, 'Hey, what about the little goat?'

'Oh, he's all right. Maybe they didn't see him in the dark.'

'That's good.'

'Well, I better go back and bury 'em. I just thought I should come and tell you and see what you thought.'

'I'm glad you came. Say hello to Lupita for me. And Margarita too.' Clay put out his hand and they shook.

'*Estcá bueno,* partner.' Tony put his foot in the stirrup, and then he turned and said, 'It sure makes you wanna kill someone, you know?'

Clay said, 'I know.'

Tony got on to the horse and rode about thirty yards. Then he turned around and came back.

Clay gave him a questioning look.

'Someone's comin',' Tony said in a low voice. 'Two men on horses.'

'The same two?'

'I don't know.' Tony slid off the horse. 'I didn't even bring a gun.'

'I doubt that we'll need one, but look in here.' Clay went to the tent and pulled back the flap. 'There's my pistol right there, and my rifle's under that coat. They're both loaded. Let's see who it is first.'

The riders were in view now. It was Thode and someone Clay didn't recognize. Clay said, 'He just keeps coming back. He won't give up till he thinks he's won.'

'Who's the other one?'

'I don't know him.'

As Thode and the other man came closer, Clay was still unable to find anything familiar about the stranger. He was a little taller in the saddle than Thode. He wore a broad-brimmed brown hat, a gray wool shirt, and leather chaps. That was the one odd detail. Most riders in this country didn't use chaps all that much in the summer. He either thought it was cold or was used to riding in brush country.

Clay said to Tony in a low voice, 'I bet they didn't expect to see you here. He probably brought his big brother for me.'

Tony nodded.

When the riders got within voice range, the stranger called

out, 'Hello the camp.'

'Come on in,' said Clay. A man's camp was supposed to extend a hundred feet from his campfire, and at least the stranger respected that.

The riders came in but did not dismount. Thode's brown eyes were expressionless. The other man's eyes, which looked light blue, had taken in the camp and were now studying Clay and Tony. The man needed a shave.

'What can I do for you?' asked Clay.

'Name's Mack,' said the stranger. 'M-A-C-K. I'm a range detective. Mr Thode is showing me around.'

'Good for him.' Clay noticed that Mack was wearing a rattlesnake-skin hatband.

'He tells me you're out of work.'

'Not for long, for as much as it's any of his business.'

'You don't seem very friendly, Mr Westbrook.'

'That might be because I don't imagine you two came here to make friends.' By now, Clay was fairly sure the man had come to pick a fight with him.

'I just came to get acquainted, so you'd know who I was.'

'I guess I do. You told me your name is Mack.'

'It is. Do you doubt it?'

'No reason to. Since you already know my name, I suppose you know my friend's name too.'

'Mr Thode said he'd had trouble with you and a Mexican. I suppose this is the one.'

Mack's eyes flickered toward Tony Campos and back to Clay.

'So you're a detective, huh?' said Tony, now that he had been more or less introduced.

'Yes, I am, for as much as it's any of your business,' said Mack, clearly mocking Clay.

'I was just wonderin', because someone killed a bunch of my sheep.'

'That don't concern me. I work for Mr Sutton.'

'I was just wonderin'.'

'Wonderin' what?'

'Why you got blood on your boot.'

Clay looked at Mack's right boot, which was pointed so that

Clay and Tony could see it right through the front of the stirrup. It had several drops of blood on it, dark now but unmistakably recent.

'You're a smart little Mexican, aren't you?'

'No, I'm a detective, too.'

Mack was obviously spoiling for a fight. He wasted no time in stepping out of the saddle, saying, 'We'll see about that.' He handed his reins back to Thode, who nudged the palomino forward and took the reins in his gloved right hand.

Tony handed his coat to Clay. Mack was wearing his gunbelt and chaps, but apparently he didn't think he needed to take them off to fight a Mexican. Clay looked at Thode, whose attention was stuck on Mack the way an owner would watch a dog or rooster going into the pit. His brown eyes were narrowed and fixed.

Mack reached out with his left, with the fist open as if he were going to cuff his opponent. Tony came in quick and drilled him four times to the face, with quick solid punches that sounded like an ax on a wet log. Mack went out from underneath his hat and landed on the ground.

Clay looked at Thode, whose eyes were widened. Thode wasn't doing anything. Then Clay looked back at Mack, wondering if he would pull his gun.

He didn't. He just got on to his hands and knees, reached out for his hat, and put it on his head as he was standing up. Taking the reins back from Thode, he said, loud enough for Clay and Tony to hear, 'That's all for today. We'll come back and finish this later.'

Thode nodded. He turned the palomino and moved it toward the river as if he were late for an appointment and had been waiting on Mack. The man in chaps, meanwhile, slapped his right leg over the saddle, reined his horse to follow Thode, and touched his hat brim as a token goodbye.

'Takes it like a sport,' said Clay as he watched the two headed for the river. 'Do you think it was him?'

'I think so, but I really don't give a damn. I hit him pretty good, didn't I?'

'Yeah, you punched him right out. He felt it. But I'd bet we're not done with that bunch yet.'

Clay took a hard look at the two riders. It didn't look like Thode was headed exactly right. Clay thought, *the fool probably doesn't know the ford. Most likely he always takes the bridge, and when he crossed here before, he followed Sutton.*

Clay walked forward to watch. Thode evidently didn't know the crossing, and Mack was following because he thought the other man did.

By now, Tony had caught on to what Clay was studying, and he walked with him.

The palomino balked at the water's edge. Thode spurred him in the flanks and slapped him on the withers with the loose ends of the reins. The horse put its front feet into the current and tried to back out. Thode spurred again and the horse went in. The front shoulders went down and then came up as the hind quarters went down. The bottom of Thode's leather vest was getting wet, and then the horse's hind end started to come back up when the horse turned in the current. Thode slapped it with the reins again, and the horse rolled. The brown vest went down under the water, and the clean white hat was carried away on the muddy current.

Clay held his breath. Thode came back up flailing and went downstream as the palomino pulled for the other side. Clay didn't see any more of Thode, but he could see the horse clearly. It charged up the other side without stopping to shake itself off, and with its head off to the left to let the reins trail free, it loped away toward the Silver Plains.

Someone should catch that horse, he thought, but I'm not going to put a hand on it.

Mack had not gone into the water. It must have been evident, as soon as the palomino's front shoulders went down, that Thode had made a blunder. Mack wheeled his horse around when Thode popped loose, and now he came galloping up the slope.

'I'm gonna try to catch him before the bridge,' he hollered.

Clay looked at Tony. 'I guess we should go help.'

Tony nodded as he put on his coat. He caught his horse and waited as Clay went into the tent for his saddle and bridle.

Clay saddled Rusty where he stood picketed. He slipped the halter off and the bridle on, flung the halter and picket rope and pin towards the campsite, and mounted up. The ground was wet and the grass would be slick. He decided he wasn't going to risk his neck for someone who was probably already drowned. He and Tony hit it at a lope and followed in the direction Mack had taken.

When they got close to the bridge they heard loud voices up ahead, then horse hoofs drumming for town. Clay and Tony turned right to catch the river just upstream of the bridge, and as they topped a rise and then headed down to the bank, they saw Mack getting off his horse with his rope in his hand.

They rode down to where Mack stood at the water's edge with the rope in his hand. He was watching the surface of the river. 'I don't see anything,' he said. 'Not even his hat.'

'Maybe one of us should go up on the bridge and watch from there,' Clay suggested.

'Probably a good idea,' Mack said, not taking his eyes off the river.

'I'll go,' Tony said, and moved out.

Clay went downstream a few yards and dismounted, then walked the horse until he was nearly under the bridge. He heard Tony's horse go up on to the bridge. He watched the river, gray in the dull afternoon. Nothing.

He heard Tony speaking to someone in Spanish. Someone must have come out from Mexican town to see what was going on.

Clay stood there at the river's edge for what seemed like a long time. He heard voices from across the river and below the bridge. It sounded like Spanish. People were coming from town now. He heard a couple of more riders thumping on to the bridge and then talking with Tony. A few minutes later, there were voices from below the bridge on his side of the river. He led his horse back upstream along the bank. Mack was talking to three men from town and still watching the surface of the water.

It was apparent that nobody expected a rescue at this point. People were there to help if needed, to watch if something exciting happened. There were no doubt some who wished to be first to spot the body.

Mack was shaking his head.

From where Clay stood at the river's edge, it all seemed distant and detached. He could not hear what Mack was saying. Nor could he make out what the people on the bridge and below it were saying, but it seemed as if they had suddenly found more to holler back and forth about. A call went out from on top of the bridge. Voices called back from below the bridge on Clay's side of the river. The man on the bridge called again. The people below were talking to one another now, short brisk noises like commands. Then a call went up. The man on the bridge hollered upstream, 'They got him.'

CHAPTER 14

Alex Thode did not have a cowboy's funeral, and he was not buried on the lone prairie. Sutton arranged to have the body shipped to Chicago on the train. The word around town was that Sutton's interests kept him from going at the moment, but he would pay his respects when he shipped cattle in the fall. There was also word that the stranger Mack had left Wyoming nearly as quickly as he came, but no matter; Sutton could find others just like him. That was the talk of the town for the next few days as Clay made his daily rounds asking if anyone was looking for hired help.

The almost total absence of opinion about Mack was interesting to Clay. If a man was brought in and called a range detective, it could mean various things. It could mean he was going to track down rustlers, primarily of cattle and horses. That was the standard meaning. It could also mean he was brought in to act as an influence, to discourage nesters from branding mavericks and to encourage small operators to mind their p's and q's, or circle-dots and slash-bar-x's. Or it could mean he was a hired gun, part bodyguard and part assassin. Mack had not been around long enough for people to define him, but he probably hadn't been tracking any suspects. Sutton had not had any reported problems with rustlers. However, until a man such as Mack became known, it would not be appropriate to make assumptions about his character, why he had come to the country, or why he had left.

Clay was convinced that Mack had come to intimidate little folks like himself and Tony, plus any other small land-holders in

Sutton's intended empire. As to why Mack left so soon, it might be partly because he was caught with blood on his boots. For his part, Sutton probably blamed Mack for not getting Thode across the river. As Clay thought about it, Sutton might really have considered Thode a friend. He certainly saw him as the son of Eastern capital, and that was more than enough to cause unhappiness.

Clay had been looking for work all week when Jackson Mead had a prospect for him. There were a couple of pilgrims, he said, who were due in town at the beginning of the next week. He was supposed to guide them up into the mountains to the French Lakes, but he could turn the job over to Clay if he wanted it. Mead said he had a trip he wanted to take, and since he hadn't even met these pilgrims yet, Clay could step in easily enough.

Being no stranger to mountain country and having been up to the French Lakes once before, Clay welcomed the chance. He talked it over with Mead in more detail and made a mental list of the provisions he would need for ten days.

Mead was also humorous about what the pilgrims expected. 'They expect you to say "palaver" and "cayuse", talk like a hermit, and use sign language. They want to see Indians and bears, and they feel like they get their money's worth if they get a good scare. You do the parts you're best at. The main thing is to have a good camp outfit.'

Clay thanked him for the advice, saying he would put the gear together right away. He said he would rather take it all out on credit than have to ask to borrow. Mead said he thought the storekeepers would let Clay have it on the cuff since he would have money as soon as he came back to town, but if he needed to borrow anything, he was welcome. Clay thanked him again and went to work at making preparations.

It was good to have work again. Camping on the river had been tolerable, but the solitude and bad weather had gotten tedious, and he simply missed working. Being alone or getting wet and miserable did not bother him if he had work to do. It was the sulking in the tent and the going up and down Main Street that had chafed him.

The outlay would be considerable, but it wouldn't be all in one place. He would need bedrolls for the two men, food for all three for ten days, and horses with gear. Besides his own he would need to lease two riding horses and three packhorses. He already had the tent, which he could let the pilgrims have to themselves if the weather was fair, and he had cooking and eating utensils. He could bring along additional warm clothing and the ax and rifle, of course. What little he didn't take he could store with Mead.

Clay was able to get everything on credit, as Mead had said. It was well known that Clay was out of work, but he knew he had a reputation for being hardworking and honest. Most of all he had the prospect of being paid right away, which made the merchants agreeable. Clay did all this business on Saturday, and to be on the safe side he stored the provisions in the livery barn where he was to pick up the horses. Then, since the weather had cleared off and the sun was warm, he went back to his camp to air out all his clothes and bedding.

The sun was warm on his back as he laid the bedding out on the woodpile and spread clothing around on the sagebrush. As he went about his work, he thought about the excursion coming up. It should do him some good – ten days away from these problems, eight of them in the mountains, and a little cash when he was done. He would clear as much in ten days as he did in a month of punching cows. If he liked the work, it might be something he could do more of.

It would be good to shake loose of Sutton for a while. He hadn't crossed trails with the land baron since that morning at the shack, but the problem still rode him like a packsaddle. He felt as if he was finally done with his grudge against Murdock, and he didn't feel as if he were transferring any more of it to his present circumstances. The business with Thode, pathetic as it had turned out to be, was at least done with. Clay didn't find in himself even a trace of resentment against Thode, and he felt sorry that the young man had ended as he had. That left Sutton, who was not likely to let go until he had everything his way.

Just before Thode's death, the owner of Silver Plains had apparently stepped up his campaign against Clay, including Tony, in what seemed to be a heavy threat. Even though a man had died, neither side had won anything, not that Clay could see. As he thought back over various run-ins they'd had, he saw that nothing had gotten resolved. It just seemed to make Sutton come back and push harder.

While he was in town, Clay had overheard one remark that let him know there might be more to come. Through most of his dealings with the townspeople he did not get an idea of what people said behind his back. He could get it from Two-Dollar Bill or Jamie Belle, but not in town. There, people might recognize that he was no longer working at the Cross Pole, but they would not say that they heard he was a troublemaker or that they heard he'd been treated like a mongrel bitch. That was the way in town – people were as civil as their storefronts.

The one crack of light had come to him in the livery barn. The young man who worked there was careless and halfway rude, but likable all the same. He was tall and not very husky, with curly blond hair and a filmy left eye. Clay had never seen him without a wad of chewing tobacco in his cheek. The young man grinned as he joshed Clay about taking out pilgrims who had never so much as 'made water or pinched a loaf' under the open sky. Then a few minutes later he tossed off a comment about Sutton blaming Clay for what had happened to Thode.

'How's that?'

'He's sayin' that if you hadn't been there, the young buck wouldn't have went under.'

Clay flared up. 'I was camped there. If I hadn't been there he might not have come by to bother me. But I never laid a hand on him that day. That fellow Mack could vouch for that. He watched Thode ride into the water.'

The young fellow spit on the stable floor. 'I don't put stock in nothin' I hear about Sutton, but that's what's goin' around, that he says you're to blame.'

Now back in his camp, as he recalled the conversation, Clay realized that Sutton was not letting up. He had found justification to keep after him, and Clay was going to have to keep looking over his shoulder.

As Clay was sorting out his winter clothes, he came to a pair of Angora chaps. He had picked them up at the end of the winter from Two-Dollar Bill, at a time when Bill was a little close and needed ten dollars. They were still in good shape. Clay shook them out. He thought he might show them to Tony and Lupita, then he decided to pack them for the trip. The dudes would have their entertainment, and he could show the chaps to his friends later on.

Sunday found Clay at the Campos household again, shamelessly in time for dinner. Tony and Margarita welcomed him as always, and Lupita gave him her hand in greeting. The women went into the kitchen, and Tony invited Clay to go out and see the garden.

The plants had grown and filled out since Clay had first seen them. It made him realize that five weeks had passed since he had first visited there. It was hard to keep track of time, kicking around as he'd had to do.

'Your garden looks great, Tony.'

'Thanks. It's a lotta work, but she's pretty.'

Clay noticed that it was neatly weeded and furrowed. Then he also saw that it had been fertilized with proceeds from the sheep pen. He thought to ask about the stock. 'How are the sheep doing?'

'Fine, fine. No more problems. The little goat, he's fine, too.' Tony paused and then said, 'I guess that one with the blood on his boots, he took off, huh?'

'That's what I heard.'

'That's good. You know, I can take it for a long time, but my sheep didn't do nothin'.'

Clay felt that Tony was making an explanation about why he hadn't been *tranquilo* a few days back. Clay said, 'You're right. We could have had more trouble from both of them over that incident, but you can't let 'em run all over you. I was right with you on it. As far as that goes, you were sticking up for me too. I think the two of them were expecting to catch me alone that day. Then with you there, that sort of turned things around on 'em.'

'Yeah, I know. But I still feel kinda bad. Maybe because I knocked the one on his ass, and then the other one goes and drowns. He was a *cabrón*, but you don't wish that somebody dies like that.'

'No, I didn't wish that on him either, but it happened, and it's not our fault.' Then he thought of the right words. 'Let's just try to put it in the past.'

Tony pushed down the corners of his mouth and nodded.

Clay went on to tell him of his plans to take the tenderfeet to the French Lakes.

'When you get back, maybe they'll have some work at the stockyards,' Tony said.

'I've asked, and they've said they don't need any help.'

'They're gonna build some more pens. They'll need somebody extra for that.'

Clay thought for a second and said, 'That might be some good work for me. I know I'd like to go back to ranch work, but that would be good for the meanwhile.'

'I'll say something to the boss. He's pretty good.'

'Thanks. I'd appreciate that.'

After dinner had been served and cleared away, while Margarita was eating and Lupita was sitting with her hands together, Tony rolled a cigarette and lit it. Then he said, 'Clay's gonna take off.'

Margarita looked up and gave a two-syllable 'No-o.' Lupita looked at him startled.

'Just for a little while,' Clay said, putting up his hands. 'I'll leave tomorrow and be back in ten days.'

'*Con el favor de Dios*,' said Margarita, nodding briefly.

Clay gave Lupita a questioning look.

'My aunt said, *con el favor de Dios*. It means, with the favor of God.'

'Oh, God willing.'

'Uh-huh. We also say, if God wants. *Sí Dios quiere*.'

'Well, anyway, I should be back in ten days.'

'He's gonna go out with some tenderfeet,' Tony said.

Margarita looked at Tony and he said something in Spanish. Margarita nodded. It occurred to Clay that Margarita, having little English, sometimes seemed simple to him. He realized he was wrong to think that. Coming at it from the other way, if he were judged on the basis of the Spanish he knew, he would seem a little more intelligent than the sugar bowl.

Clay said, 'Visitors. They want to go to the mountains, so I got the job of takin' 'em.'

'That's good,' said Margarita. 'Are they your family?'

'No, I've never met 'em. It's work.'

'Oh,' she said. 'They gonna pay. That's good.'

Clay looked at Lupita and said, 'I'll take my tent, and it'll be my job to run a camp for 'em. I'll be a guide.'

'Well, I hope you have a good trip,' Lupita answered. 'I hope you go to pretty places and see all the nice things. And I hope you enjoy it. I hope the other people, your customers, enjoy it. How many are they?'

'Two. Two men. They want to see the country. Sightseers.'

'Oh.' She nodded.

'I'm not leaving till tomorrow,' he said.

She smiled.

When Margarita got up to go to the kitchen, Tony said he was going to have a siesta. Clay and Lupita sat at the table. She was wearing a pale red dress that brought out her brown skin and dark hair. Clay felt soft, like he was moving around inside himself. 'Can you go out?' he asked.

'Do you want to go to see the river?'

'Not today,' he said. He had already thought about it, and he wanted more time to put Thode's drowning in the past. 'Can we just walk outside?'

'I think so. Let me talk to my aunt.' She was gone a few minutes and then came back, shifting her head as she draped the black shawl in front of her shoulders. It struck Clay that there was a real womanness about her, something unconscious in her movement and presence. Her face beamed. 'Ready?'

'How about Marcos?'

'He doesn't have to go if we just go in the street.'

'Oh.'

Clay put on his hat as they went out into the sunny afternoon. They crossed the street toward the shade, then walked slowly. He moved so that she was on the right, farther from the street, as he had learned to walk with a woman.

'I'm supposed to walk on the outside. Do you do it that way, too?'

'Oh, yes. You do it right.'

People appeared at the doorways, casually. They were people who had seen Clay before and were getting another look.

'People are the same, aren't they?' he said.

'Excuse me?'

'I said, people are the same. Wherever you go. Neighbors are curious.'

She laughed. 'Oh, yes. They want to look and then they want to talk about it.'

'Nothing bad, I hope.'

'No, I don't think so. Sometimes they tell my aunt it's not good, that I shouldn't go out with someone who isn't one of us.'

'What does she say?'

'She knows you're different, but she says there are good and bad people where we come from, and here too.'

Clay nodded. He had felt very welcome in the Campos house, and he had never felt judged. At this moment, however, he felt as if he had passed some kind of inspection without knowing it, and he was glad to realize that her family saw merit in him.

Then he thought of a good question. 'What does your uncle say?'

'They say the same thing. They think the same.'

'Sometimes it seems like he talks to me less than he would if he, or if I – let me see how to say this – if I wasn't so interested in you.'

'Oh, he has to be that way. He would do the same thing with any other boy.'

'Then I'm glad it's me,' he said. He looked at her, and they both smiled broadly as they walked along.

A little boy and a little girl crossed in front of them, running. Lupita greeted a woman who was standing outside her door. The woman returned the greeting. Clay nodded. He was embarrassed because he couldn't remember if he had talked to that woman when he was asking for directions the first day. As he and Lupita walked, he realized he had nodded to several of these people before as he came and went, but since he was a foreigner, they didn't expect him to know anyone.

They came to the end of the street and curved around to the next street going back. They crossed into the shade, and Clay moved to Lupita's right.

'I'm going to miss you,' he said.

'I'm going to miss you, too,' she said. 'But you'll come back, *con el favor de Dios.*' She looked at him sideways and smiled.

'Uh-huh. I'm learning.'

They walked to the north end of the street without saying anything more. He wondered how many times they could make the loop.

'Do we just keep going around?'

'If you like.'

When they came to the south end of the street again, he noticed a bench outside the church building, on the shady side.

'Can we sit there?' he asked.

'Sure.'

'Let's go around one more time. Then we can sit down.'

They didn't speak to one another as they made another round. Lupita greeted people she hadn't spoken to on the first time around. Clay noticed the woman sweeping the flat stones in front of her house. Children skipped past them; dogs came out and sniffed him. They they were back at the south end of the street, sitting on the bench. They sat so that he had the little town on his left side and Lupita on his right. Between them their hands joined.

'I thought a lot about our conversation last week,' he said.

'Yes. . . .'

'And it all makes sense. I can see that it's in the past. I don't feel stuck to it any more.'

'That's good.'

Clay thought about her phrase for a moment. *That's good.* He had noticed it came frequently in conversation with Tony and Margarita as well as with Lupita. It seemed to be the equivalent of Tony's *está bueno.* It probably had more than one equivalent in Spanish that in English all came out sounding the same. It seemed to Clay that the person used this one phrase to show agreement and encouragement and to keep things moving forward.

Then he said, 'I wanted to tell you before I left how I was thinking about these things.'

She squeezed his hand.

'You know, I've listened to what you've had to say about not wanting to have trouble all the time. That makes sense, too. I mean, I don't want to have any trouble. Not just because you don't, but because it's better to live without it.'

She reached with her right hand and caressed his right forearm once, then rested her hand there.

'You know that we had some more trouble the other day, and I'm sorry it turned out the way it did. I hope I'm close to the end of it.' He looked at her, and their eyes met. Then he went on. 'I wanted to tell you before I left that I'm going to try to stay away from trouble and hope it comes to an end. And I'm not just saying it because I think you want to hear it. I'm serious. I want everything to be *tranquilo*. For me, and for you and me.'

Their eyes met. He lifted his right arm and put it around her shoulders. Then their lips met in a warm, moist kiss that seemed like standing at the top of a mountain and swimming at the bottom of a pool.

They drew apart and straightened back into their earlier positions.

'People are probably watching,' she said.

'I know, but I had to tell you that, and I couldn't tell you without things happening like that.'

'I know,' she said, smiling.

He kissed her quick, just face to face, and sat back like before. 'No one saw that,' he said, winking.

She laughed.

Their hands were together again, his right and her left. He took a breath as if to speak, then turned to her. She gave him a look that said, go ahead.

'This is hard to say. But when I'm with you, I feel clean. Everything seems right. I want to do things right.'

Their eyes met and she nodded.

He went on. 'Sometimes, things seem like they weigh a ton. Everything seems tangled up. But when I'm with you, the weight is gone and everything seems straightened out. I want to be able to keep feeling that way.'

She pressed his hand and said, 'That's good. I want you to

come back.'

'I hope so. Now, the other part of it is, I want you to feel like things are better when I'm around.'

'They are.'

'I mean all the time. I remember what you said about your mother, and how she took on your father's troubles, and how you didn't want to live that way.'

'That's right.'

'That's what I mean. I don't want my life to be one long fight, and I don't want to make it that way for someone else.'

They sat for a while without speaking, and he was afraid he had gone too far. He sensed that she had something to say, so he waited.

Finally she said, 'It's a long trip you're taking. Will it be dangerous?'

'There's always dangers, like a horse losing its footing, or a bear thinking he wants the bacon. But as for this other trouble, I don't think so. You never know, of course, but I wouldn't want you to worry about it.'

'Be careful.'

'I'll be careful. I promise you.'

'We say, *Dios te ayude.*'

'Say it again?'

'*Dios te ayude.* It means may God help you.'

'Sort of like God be with you or God bless you.'

'We say those, too, but this is the one we say when a person goes away.'

'And what do I say?'

'*Gracias.*'

CHAPTER 15

The two pilgrims, as Jackson Mead called them, were scheduled to arrive before noon on Monday. Mead suggested that he and Clay meet them together as they got off the train. Then they would be left in their new guide's hands. Clay thought it was a good idea; the pilgrims hadn't met their original guide, so they probably wouldn't have any objections to the change. However, Mead thought it best to do things personally, so they did. The Easterners, who seemed somewhat dizzy just from getting off the train, didn't seem to have the slightest disagreement with the plan. When Mead assured them that Clay would treat them just as well as he would have done, they nodded blankly.

Clay had the packs laid out at the livery barn, so all he had to do was include the gentlemen's bags, load the pack-horses, saddle the riding horses, and get the expedition underway.

The two men were likable from the very start. They were about Clay's age, and brothers. One was a painter and one was a writer. They had come out from Philadelphia to 'gather impressions,' as they said. Charles Sanders, the older of the two, was the painter, and Arthur was a writer. They hoped to collaborate on a series of magazine articles as well as develop material for individual projects. Exuberant about their adventure, they were reluctant to go to the café while Clay got the horses ready, but he advised them to get a bite and freshen up, as he would be a while. They were interested in the details. Clay assured them they would see the packing and the unpacking a few more times, in more interesting places, when they could also help. Right now he had a helper in the person of the young man who worked in the livery barn.

An hour later, they were out on the trail. The two brothers rode on Clay's left, while the packhorses were strung out behind him. Clay observed the men as they rode along. They were of middle height and middle build, and they resembled one another closely. They had dark brown wavy hair and sidewhiskers, dark eyes, and narrow faces. If there was a notable difference, it was that the younger one was a shade heavier in all aspects.

The brothers chatted quite a bit. Frequently one would draw the other's attention to some detail they were passing, and they would talk it over. They also had a large fund of shared humor. A word or two would mean a joke they had been through before, no doubt more than once. They both did imitations of other voices, and sometimes they would mimic the same voice. When a meadowlark fluttered away, Charles said in a brogue, 'Ay, lookit the wee berd.' A few minutes later, when a bony jackrabbit started up and then paused fifty yards away with its haunches toward the travelers, Arthur said in the same brogue, 'Ach, he's pur as a crow.'

The party followed an easy trail all that afternoon and into the early evening. The trail ran parallel to the river on the north side, higher up with a good view. From time to time, Clay would look over his shoulder and see how the packhorses were traveling. When he thought everyone could use a breather, he'd call a rest. At that time he would check the loads, straighten any that had shifted, and tighten the lashes as needed.

Clay found a likely campsite about two hours before dark. It had wood, water, and grass. He planned to follow the river through part of the following morning, cross a wooden bridge, and head southwest to the mountains. Even now they were in the shadow of the peaks.

The tenderfeet helped Clay unload the horses. Then, since they seemed to have stiffened up from several hours in the saddle, Clay told them to relax while he set up camp. He stripped the horses and picketed them, unpacked the ax, and rustled up some firewood.

'I've got a tent,' he told his guests, 'but I don't think I'll go to the bother of cutting poles and setting it up for just one night.' He looked at the sky. 'I think we can get by. Once we get into the mountains, though, we'll need it.'

The other two nodded. Arthur was writing in a notebook, and Charles was drawing on a sketch pad. They were easy to get along with.

The campsite had been used before. Clay got a fire going in the firepit and laid out what he would need for supper. He had fresh meat for the first night. After that it was salt pork and whatever camp meat he could bring down. He set the bedrolls nearby so he could roll them out by the fire later on. As the fire blazed he remembered the new canvas bucket, so he dug it out and filled it at the river, then hung it from the stub of a tree branch.

As it got darker, Charles brought his sketch pad over next to

127

the campfire so he could continue by firelight. From the tilt of the pad, Clay could see the picture. It was a portrait of a Western character, in a hat. Then Clay looked closer, and he recognized the rock-hard features of Sutton. It startled him.

'Who's that?' he asked.

'Just someone who was in the café.'

'Did he talk to you?'

'No, he just stared at us at great length, so I got a good look at his face.'

'That's pretty good from memory.'

'He had a memorable face.'

'Uh-huh.'

'It usually comes out better, in an actual portrait, if I have the subject in front of me. But I'm looking for local color, universals and particulars, and I don't intend to present this as a portrait, so this is fine.' He held it out. 'Quite usable, actually.'

An image came to Clay's mind. 'Say,' he said, 'would you think about doing one for me when we get back?'

'I could think about it. Who's the subject?'

Clay hesitated, wondering how he should say it. He hadn't actually used a term for Lupita before. 'I've got a . . . girl back at town that would make a beautiful portrait. She's got long dark hair, and dark eyes.'

Charles nodded as if he'd heard it before.

'And she's got beautiful brown skin. I don't know if you could catch the color with a pencil, but maybe with shading—'

'Indian?'

'Um, no. She's Mexican.'

Charles raised his eyebrows and wagged his head back and forth, as if in thought. 'That could be interesting, too. We'll see how we're fixed for time when we get back.'

'I hope it works out. She's beautiful.'

'Oh, I believe it.'

After supper, Arthur brought out a straight-stemmed pipe and loaded it up. When he lit it, he sent forth a cloud of aromatic smoke. Pipe in hand, he made a straight, closed-mouth smile. 'Now,' he said, 'a little snakebite medicine, and we have all the comforts a savage camp can provide.' He brought out a silver, pint-sized flask and offered it to his brother, who uncapped it and took a sip. He handed it to Clay. 'Brandy. Heap good.'

Clay laughed. 'No, thanks.' Then he thought, if there were any genuinely hostile savages around, the aroma of the pipe tobacco would have had them all scalped by now.

As the next hour passed, Clay noticed that Arthur drank the larger share of the brandy and stared at the fire, while Charles enjoyed leaning back on his rolled-up bed and gazing at the stars. As their talk wandered, Clay learned that Charles had a fiancée back at home. He was going to marry her when he got back.

Con el favor de Dios, Clay thought. Then he asked Arthur if he was married.

'Nope,' he said, squinting at the fire reflected on the flask. 'She cast her love away upon another man.'

'Shakespeare?' said Charles, perking up in mimicry of an Englishman.

'Sanders,' said Arthur, continuing the scholarly tone. 'Shakespeare puts it thus: `When my love swears that she is made of truth—'

' "I do believe her, though I know she lies",' Charles rejoined.

Clay nodded and smiled. There had been a time when it wouldn't have been funny.

Morning came clear and calm. Clay built up the fire, took the horses to water, and put on a pot of coffee. The tenderfeet rolled out cheerful and got dressed. It was going to be another good day, Clay thought. He doubted that dude wrangling would always be this much fun.

As they got into the mountains, it became evident that the Easterners were quite taken with the idea that they were going to the French Lakes. The brothers began speaking to each other in French. Clay could not understand what they were saying, but he could tell they were joshing each other.

At one point, when they reached a crest of the foothills and paused before the timbered mountains, Arthur declared, '*Nous voulons voir les Tetons!*'

Clay looked at him.

'*Nous voulons voir les Tetons!*' he declaimed more fiercely, with a glaring eye.

Clay shook his head and looked at Charles.

'He says we want to see the Tetons.'

'They're damn near four hundred miles away.'

'*Les Tetons*!' repeated Arthur, cupping his hands beneath his breasts.

'Oh, that,' said Clay, remembering the humor. 'We all want to see them.'

They went on, up into the otherworld of the mountains. Sometimes the trail was broad, leading over the backs of grassy ridges. At other times it led through timber, across green meadows where the blue lupine bloomed, and across sparkling creeks. Toward late afternoon they hit a slow climb along the side of a mountain, a narrow ledge with a steep drop-off to the left. Clay looked back over his shoulder every few minutes to see how the packs were riding and to see how the boys were taking it. They seemed to be gathering impressions well enough, clutching their saddle horns and gazing wide-eyed into the canyon below.

When they came out on level ground, the group stopped to take a blow. Clay got off to check the packs, and the dudes got down to walk around.

'Terrific!' said Charles. 'Just terrific!'

'Really impressive,' added Arthur.

'We'll see more,' Clay said. 'We'll camp in about another hour, and then we'll go higher up tomorrow.'

The brothers nodded to each other. They were clearly appreciating what they had come to see.

Clay set their camp near a spring that came out of the side of the mountain. The water was clear and cold, sweet to the taste. The smell of the pines, mixed with the cold thin air, made a man happy. This was really living, up and away from all the complications. He could see why Jackson Mead chose this line of work. Who wouldn't rather hear the wind in the pines than the whistle of a steam engine?

The pilgrims were good helpers in camp. They gave a hand at setting up the tent and carrying firewood. Clay told them they could have the tent and he would sleep outside unless the weather got bad, so they laid out their gear while he sliced bacon and mixed biscuit dough.

That evening around the campfire, Arthur lit his pipe again and brought out his flask, which he had apparently refilled from a reserve. After a while he remarked that it was colder tonight.

'That stuff makes you feel it,' said Clay, nodding at the flask, 'but it sure is. There'll be snow on the ground when we get up higher.'

During the middle of the next day they reached the place where Clay wanted to set up the main camp. There was a spring, timber with deadfall, and grass for the horses.

'We'll be here a few days,' he said. 'You'll have plenty of time to wander around. The lakes are up higher, just below timberline. There are two lakes together. If you want, we can go up there on foot after we pitch camp and get a bite to eat.'

They unpacked the horses and set up the tent. Clay showed the boys how to cut small pine branches to cover the floor before they rolled out their beds. While they were at that task he staked out the horses, made a pile of all the saddles and tack, and covered it with a canvas from the load. This was a good camp. He shaped up a firepit and gathered up an armful of firewood; then with a fire going he heated some canned beans. Tomorrow, when time spread out, he would see about some meat. After that he would cook a pot of the dry beans he had packed. He also had rice, pork, dried fruit, canned tomatoes, flour – plenty of good grub.

The French Lakes provided just the kinds of impressions the two brothers had come to find. The lakes were a satin blue against green grass and darker green timber, with snowbanks still holding on in the deep shady spots. The mountain rose behind them, giving way to gray rock outcroppings and then white, snowcapped ridges. The vast sky was blue and cloudless.

'On top of the world,' Arthur said.

'There's plenty of mountains that are higher,' said Clay, 'but you can't see 'em from here.'

'This is absolute freedom,' said Charles. 'A hundred miles from nowhere, and all to ourselves. I would love to bring Betty here. She'd love it, too.'

Clay nodded. 'I bet she would.'

They gazed for a while, quietly, each of them off by himself.

Clay thought, it really did feel like the top of the world, like a person could fly. Someday, when they no longer needed a chaperone, he would like to bring Lupita to this place.

On the way back down, the brothers were back to chatting and joking again, pausing to point out a perspective. Charles was also interested in rocks, so he frequently picked one up, turned it over in the sunlight, then set it back down where he had found it. At one turn in the trail they could see over the trees and down into their camp. The white tent and the brown horses stood out against the green meadow. It was a satisfying sight and a good camp to go back to.

Arthur evidently thought so, too. 'That's a good scene,' he said. His brother nodded, and the two of them stood for a long moment, studying it.

That evening, just before rustling the evening meal, Clay brought out the angora chaps. The dudes were delighted, especially Charles, who asked Clay to put them on and strike some poses. Then he hung them on the corner of the tent nearest the fire and made sketches of them.

In the morning, Clay was up before dawn and out of camp while the brothers were still sleeping. His plan was to try to find a deer, a yearling or young buck that wouldn't have a fawn. These nights would be good for hanging meat, and the three of them would eat the better part of a small deer in a week. He cut across the meadow north of camp, past the horses, and into the timber.

He intended to come out by the lakes, across from where they had stood the afternoon before. Halfway there, as he came to a clearing he paused as usual. There on the sunny side of the opening was a young forked-horn buck, grazing. Clay saw the small antlers, in velvet now, and he decided it was the animal to take. It was less than a hundred yards away, facing left and giving a broadside. Clay moved behind an aspen tree, rested his left hand and the forearm of the rifle against the tree trunk, and took aim. When he pulled the trigger, the deer lurched and bolted. It ran about forty yards to the edge of the timber and went down, front first.

Clay went to the fallen deer and looked down at it where it lay right side up. He had made a good shot, as he could tell from the dark red blood where the bullet had come out. Leaning his rifle against a small aspen, he took out his jackknife and opened it. Then he rolled the deer on to its back, stepped over a hind leg to hold it still, and began to field-dress the animal. This was a good deer, he thought as he trimmed out the entrails. Their camp would make good use of it.

The tenderfeet had heard the shot and were outside of the tent, dressed, when Clay got back to camp. Both of them observed him as he walked toward them, and their gaze was drawn toward the bloody hands and the rifle.

Charles asked, 'Come into some luck?'

'I sure did. We've got meat on the ground. Let me put this rifle away and wash my hands, and I'll get a horse to drag him in. Do you fellows want to go along?'

They both did, of course, since a dead deer was an impression worth gathering. At the site of the kill, Clay showed them the black tail and antlers, the main features that distinguished the Western mule deer from the Eastern whitetail. 'It's a small one,' he said, pulling Rusty's head around to make sure the horse knew what was up. Then he looped his rope over the velvet antlers, tied the rope to the saddle horn, and got Rusty to pulling.

By the time he had the deer back to camp, hoisted up on a pine branch, and skinned, it was mid-morning. Arthur took interest in the whole process and paid close attention. Charles, meanwhile, built up the fire and let it burn back to coals for cooking. There was bacon grease in the skillet from the night before, so Clay put the skillet over the coals and sliced deer liver for their late breakfast.

They ate the rich meat, which the dudes described as 'not entirely delicious' but 'part of the adventure.' Arthur said he found it all intriguing and would like to come back sometime to hunt.

'We'll get you a nicer one than that,' said Clay. 'He's a good little fellow for camp meat, nice and chubby, but if you come for a real hunt, say in October or November of a year, we'll find his big brother for you.'

Camp was as jolly as ever. The three young men drank a pot of coffee and watched the shadows move as the sun climbed in the sky. Charles and Arthur said they'd like to go on a hike, so Clay offered to take them around the mountain to the southwest to see a canyon. He said they would be back in time for an early supper of venison steak. The boys were all for it, so Clay put together a bag of dried fruit and cold biscuits, and they were off.

The two brothers liked to walk. As Charles put it, one could appreciate the scenery more if one worked to get there. Clay took them to the rim of the canyon, which they declared to be 'stupendous,' 'spectacular,' and 'sublime.' They had brought their notebooks, so after their initial wonderment they sat down to write and sketch. Clay found a soft shady spot to lie back. He scooted his hat over his eyes and spent a pleasant hour or more, enjoying the peacefulness and thinking about Lupita.

He awoke to something pulling on the toe of his boot. He pushed up his hat and saw Charles crouching there. 'Sun's slipping towards the yardarm,' he said.

Clay got up and stretched, and then the three of them headed back in the direction of camp. The tenderfeet turned and looked back at the canyon, lingered, and then joined their guide.

Coming back through the last stand of timber before camp, Clay smelled something burning. 'I don't like that smell,' he said.

When they walked out of the timber, they saw why there was a stench in the air. The tent was collapsed, and smoke was coming up from it. Drawing closer, Clay saw the dirty work. Someone had yanked out the tent poles and then, apparently with the short-handled camp shovel, had put a heap of coals in the middle of the pile. It was a clear act of malice. Whoever had done it had taken the time to make a good bed of coals and then ruin as much gear as possible in one spot. The heap of coals had burned through the tent canvas and into the bedrolls below.

'Look here,' said Arthur, pointing at the firepit.

'The sons of bitches,' said Clay. Someone had raked the remaining coals together and dropped the angora chaps on to them, hair down.

Clay looked up and around. They hadn't taken the horses. Taking them would be rustling, good for thirteen turns on a slipknot. Besides, whoever had done this would have known that five of the horses weren't his. On the other hand, the deer carcass was gone. Only a slashed remnant of Clay's good rope was left tied to the tree where he had hung the venison.

'I don't see any humor in this at all,' said Charles. He looked at his brother and then at Clay, who was obviously the target of the attack. 'I say we get the hell out of here.'

CHAPTER 16

Clay looked over his shoulder as he led the way down the last ridge out of the mountains. The three light-loaded packhorses were traveling well, and the two pilgrims were not lagging. By Jackson Mead's formula they should feel they had gotten their money's worth, having gotten a good scare, but Clay felt bad about the whole sorry mess. The brothers were being good sports about it. Clay had put together some beds for them. He split his own bedroll, which had been overlooked, and then he added some salvaged tent canvas and some saddle blankets. For his own bed he rolled up in manties, the canvas sheets he used for wrapping and covering the loads. Although the two adventurers remained good-natured, their trip was ruined. They agreed to pay one-third of the original cost if Clay could get them to the train in two days flat. By Clay's figuring, he could pay the cost of the horses, which would be less now, and the food. He would be in debt for the dry goods, mainly bedding and pack supplies, and he was out of a tent.

As a parting favor for the visitors, Clay left them at a train station not far from the bridge where they had crossed the river on the way out. That way, he saved them the last four hours on horseback. The two brothers shook hands with Clay and waved goodbye from the platform, but nothing more was said about future visits.

With three saddle horses to switch off on and the pack-horses even lighter, Clay made good time on the last part of the trip. He pulled into the livery barn with his empty caravan at about seven o'clock on Saturday evening. The young man showed surprise at seeing him.

'Whoa! I didn't expect to see you till the middle of next week. Did your dudes quit on you?'

'They finished ahead of schedule,' said Clay, having decided to say no more than necessary for the time being.

'I hope you came out ahead, then.'

'Not enough to brag about.'

'By the way, there's a message for you.'

'A letter?'

'No, just a message. Your friend Sutton left word that he'd like to talk business with you.'

Clay felt dead tired. 'When did he come by?'

'He didn't. One of his riders did, a few hours ago. There's a few of them in town tonight. I told him I didn't expect to see you for a few days.'

'Let me think.' Clay leaned against his saddle. He breathed out heavily and said, 'Oh, hell, I might as well get it over with. If they come back, tell 'em I'll be out on my homestead tomorrow morning.'

'I can get that word to 'em.'

Clay thought it over some more as he and the stable boy unpacked and unsaddled the five horses. He had very little left, but it was too much to carry on a horse he was going to ride. After getting permission to leave a few things at the livery barn, he tied his bedroll on the back of the saddle and rode out. The sun was slipping in the west. It wasn't sundown yet, but it would be before long.

The last month had been exhausting. Little by little it had worn him down. He had a handful of things back at the livery and another handful at Mead's, and that was it, but he felt scattered out. He didn't have a roof to sleep under or a place to shelter his saddle and rifle. All he had was a bare piece of ground, and he was going to go there to sleep. If he felt just as low in the morning, he would give in.

Sutton was out to crush him, that was all. The man wanted to reduce him to nothing and then buy him out. He had probably gotten Clay fired at the Cross Pole, with Highpockets' help, and now he had ruined Clay's next source of income. He had no doubt found out where the tenderfeet were headed and had then

136

sent some henchmen to watch until the three were gone from camp. They must have been watching the night before and must have seen the pantomime with the chaps, or they wouldn't have been so deliberate in that detail. By now Sutton would know that Clay was flat and might be willing to deal.

Like before, Clay had no fear that Sutton would try to rub him out. There had been plenty of opportunities, and the land baron was being open about the meeting. Sutton wanted to talk business. Well, maybe they'd talk.

In spite of how worn-out he felt, or maybe because of it, he didn't sleep well. There was a quarter moon, and he could see his saddle dumped on the prairie beside him. A hundred yards away, his horse grazed at the end of the stake rope. That was what he had – that, plus a rifle and an ax, a tin bucket and a canvas one, a few pots and pans, and his clothes. Some scraps of canvas and a few days' worth of grub. He looked at the moon and the stars and he thought, it was a wonderful life. Why fight? He could give in and go get another homestead somewhere else, maybe even on the other side of the river. Kick this one in the ass.

He slept for a while, then was awake, slept a while longer, and woke up again. Finally at dawn he rolled out, went to the creek to wash his face, and came back to sit on his bed-roll. As he watched his horse grazing in the sunrise he thought, I should feel free at a time like this, and I don't.

When he took the horse to water, he saw a flock of magpies flying over, half a dozen of them. They were probably on their way to a breakfast they knew about. After returning the horse to its picket, he went back and stretched out on his bedroll. That was how big a piece of ground he had been cut down to, he thought – a piece of prairie the size of a grave. That was the way the song went: '. . . In a narrow grave, just six by three. Bury me not on the lone prairie.'

Rusty nickered and Clay woke up. The sun was higher now, and there were three riders coming from the south. Clay was wearing his six-gun and had the rifle at hand in his bedding, but he doubted he would need either. If Sutton wanted to talk business, he had probably brought a couple of bodyguards just to keep it safe for him.

Sutton rode the last two hundred yards by himself. Clay was standing out in the open so he could move around easily to avoid looking into the sun. Sutton didn't do any maneuvering. He stopped the bay horse a few yards from Clay and then, to Clay's surprise, he dismounted.

'Good morning,' he said, but made no movement toward shaking hands.

'Good morning.'

'I came to see if you were ready to talk sense.' Sutton's face was blunt and hard. As before, he acted as if the past hadn't happened the way it had.

Clay resented the act. 'Last time we talked, you told me I didn't have a claim on this land. I do. You were the one who didn't make sense.'

'I think Alex made a mistake. He thought he had a claim on this piece.' The gray eyes flickered.

'And then somebody burned me out.' Clay glanced at the black heap to his right.

Sutton looked past him. 'I couldn't tell you anything about that. I have enough to do to watch my own place.'

'I bet.'

'You don't have to get surly with me, Westbrook. I came to offer to buy your homestead. I believe you that you have a claim to it.' Sutton drew the ends of the reins through his free left hand.

'You must think I'm ready to sell.'

'Look at you. Just a saddle tramp. Not a pot to piss in or a window to throw it out of.' Sutton made a dry spit with his tongue and lips, as if trying to get rid of a particle.

'What do you know about what I have or don't have?'

'Just look at you.' Sutton motioned with his left hand.

Clay realized he had been in the same clothes for a week and had slept in them for half the nights during that time. He was the ragtail, standing by his saddle and bed out on a bare piece of ground.

'Why can't you just leave me alone?'

'I could, but I can make better use of this land than you can. You can't make a living off it anyway. Not like it is.'

138

'I'll do all right.'

'To tell you the truth, I don't want a bunch of snotty little half-breeds out here, either.'

Clay got in the first punch, a good solid right to the jaw, but Sutton didn't flinch. He just dropped his reins and came at Clay like a bear. Clay ducked and punched with his left. He connected, but Sutton kept at him. He felt Sutton's arms around him, then his jacket pulled up over his head, knocking off his hat and holding his arms out straight. Sutton clubbed him with a right, hitting him on the left shoulder and side of the head and knocking him to the ground.

When he landed, Clay rolled over and pulled the jacket the rest of the way off as he rose to his feet. Sutton was coming at him. He punched the big man with all of his force, driving a right to the midsection. Sutton stopped but did not fold. Clay punched upward with his left and connected again, but still he couldn't budge the man. He thought, *maybe he's dazed.* Clay backed out and then came right back in to punch him again, but Sutton brought his right arm around quickly and clubbed Clay on the side of the head. Clay staggered backward but stayed on his feet.

Sutton had taken some good punches and had to have felt them. He probably didn't want to take any more, and since he had gotten in the last good one, he was in a position to quit. He said, 'Damn you, you pup. I'm through talkin' to you.' He turned and walked to his horse, which had moved back several yards.

Clay could see the other two riders closer now. They had moved in a hundred yards and stopped. Clay didn't recognize either of them.

Then he called out to Sutton. 'Go to hell and stay there, Sutton. I don't care if it takes me a year, or two years, or more, but I'll be back on this land. And I'll prove up on it.'

Sutton didn't answer. He just mounted up, turned and gave Clay a cold, blocky stare, and rode away.

Clay picked up his hat and jacket and dusted them off. He put the hat on his head and watched Sutton ride to the other two riders. They turned their horses around, and the three rode off to the south. Clay thought, *I almost sold it to him. If he had had a little more control and not made that crack, I probably would have sold.*

That was his mistake.

Clay worked his right hand open and closed. It had been like a rock wall. He hadn't lost and he hadn't won. He had just thrown himself at a wall, that was all.

He knelt and rolled up his bedding. That was about it for this place, for right now. At this point he was in debt enough. Even if he could borrow to build again, it was more than he wanted to owe the world. He would go to work for wages, get another stake, and be back like he said he would.

As he saddled the horse he realized he wasn't worked up. He was calm. He had gone up against the wall and now he was done with it. He knew it was going to be hard for either of them to get satisfaction in this conflict, and he could live with that knowledge as he waited for Sutton's next move. Meanwhile, he could go into town, spend two bits on a long hot bath in the barbershop, and spend Sunday afternoon the way he liked to.

Lupita was wearing the lightweight white dress and had her hair tied back in a ponytail. Clay hadn't seen it that way before, but he liked it. When she reappeared a few minutes later, she had it down around her shoulders as usual. It bounced and waved as she walked from the room back into the kitchen.

Margarita came out of the kitchen. '*Clé!*' she exclaimed. She came to the table and reached across it. He rose and took her hand. 'I always happy that you come to my house,' she said.

'I'm always happy to be here.'

Tony said, 'You always take us by surprise. One time you don't come, another time you come back early.'

Lupita had come back into the room. She and Margarita were standing, and Tony was sitting. Clay had a sense of an audience.

'I got finished early with the tenderfeet. Someone came and wrecked our camp, burned the tent and beds.'

'*¡Ay qué malo! Pura venganza,*' said Margarita.

'Is that "vengeance"?' asked Clay.

'Yeah,' Tony answered. 'Like the family trouble.'

Clay remembered the story, of course. 'That's what it was. Spite.'

'So the tenderfeet took off, huh?' asked Tony.

'That was it. I couldn't blame them. They could see I was bad company.'

'They come by train?' asked Tony.

'Yeah. They're on their way back now. I got into town last night.' Then he thought, might as well tell the rest and get done with it. 'So I went out to my place and slept there. Bigwig Sutton came by this morning, and we had a set-to.'

'A fight?' asked Tony.

'A little bit of one. Not much. Mainly, he wanted to buy my land and I said no.'

Tony said nothing as he looked at the table.

Clay said, 'I guess I've just got to build back up. Get a job, pay off what I owe, then try to save some money to build another house. It might take a year or two, but I've got five years.'

'Sure,' said Tony. 'You're young. You're like new.'

Clay laughed. 'Sometimes I don't feel that way.' Then he met eyes with Lupita and he felt himself blushing. 'Just sometimes,' he said.

When the meal was over, Clay recognized what seemed to be the pattern on his last couple of visits. The boys went outside as always, Margarita went to the kitchen, Tony went for a nap, and the young couple was left to talk. As they sat there without saying anything, Clay appreciated Lupita's presence all over again. He thought that's what they called a woman's intuition. A woman didn't have to ask much or say much, but it all got taken care of. Maybe not all women, he thought, since he'd known so few, but Lupita certainly had that fine quality. That was why things worked.

She was sitting around the corner of the table from him, and she laid her left hand on his right. 'You look serious,' she said.

'Thinking about us.' Then, so she wouldn't think he was going too far, he said, 'I wonder sometimes why you care for me. I know why I'm crazy about you, but what about you? What do you see in me?'

He wanted to hear her say, 'You're brave and handsome,' but what he heard was just as good, if not better.

'You're responsible and honest. You respect me. Actually, you respect all of us, my family, and that's important.'

Clay raised his index finger and touched her fingers, bump-bump-bump like a washboard. As her answer sunk in, he realized it told him something about himself and something about her – what he was like and what she valued – but those things weren't separate. They ran together, blended. It was more what he was like in response to her and what she was like in return. It was the mutual understanding that Jackson Mead had talked about, and it had come about naturally.

Then he asked, 'Do you still think God wanted us to meet?'

'Nothing happens if God doesn't want it.'

'Even the bad things?' He thought of her father and mother, of Tony and Margarita's babies.

'Yes, the bad things too. Maybe we can't understand, but it's what God wants.' She looked at their hands as she spoke.

Clay couldn't push away a worry that kept coming back. He said, 'Do you think it's a problem if I don't see God exactly the way you do?'

'Do you believe in God?'

'Well, yes. Of course.'

'And it's not a problem if I don't believe exactly the same way?'

'No, of course not.'

She looked at him. 'It would be a problem if a man wanted a woman to leave the church. But I know you're not that way.'

'No, I'm not.'

'Then it's not a problem.'

Clay wanted to blurt, then how will we get married? How will our children be raised? But he didn't. He knew that she knew that he meant those things, and he sensed her assurance that if and when they came to those questions, there would be a solution.

He rubbed his thumb over the top of her fingers. There could be problems from time to time, he thought. Two ways of doing things, two traditions. It could cause friction. Then he thought, she accepted him and his ways just as he accepted her and hers. He could enjoy the graceful ways of leaving the room or of talking about a trip he planned to take. He could live with her view that God wanted people to suffer, or that if people suffered, God wanted it. He could live with her.

Then he thought of the remarks he'd heard from people like Two-Dollar Bill and Sutton – people who didn't want to see a mix. There would be people like that, some more polite than others, and there could be friction with them. Jackson Mead had mentioned that, too. There might be some places where he wouldn't be invited – some houses, maybe some jobs – but he wouldn't miss them, especially when he had the places where he would be welcome. He was at home where he was sitting right now. He raised her hand and bent to kiss it. Quietly. She smiled.

A clatter came from the kitchen, and it made him aware of the silence. He spoke up. 'It's a good day for a walk, don't you think?'

'Which way would you like to go?' She released his hand.

He made a horizontal circle with his right index finger.

'Like last week?' she asked.

'If you'd like.'

She nodded. 'Let me go tell my aunt.'

After two rounds in the little village, greeting the neighbors and being noticed, Clay and Lupita sat again on the bench in the shadow of the church.

'It's a pretty day,' she said. 'Calm and peaceful.' She dabbed her cheek with the gray shawl and then pushed it back on her shoulders.

'Yes, it is. Especially with you. You always make me feel that way.'

She looked down at their hands, joined between them, and he noticed her lovely eyelashes.

'I have a question,' he said.

'Yes?' She looked up.

'Time for another lesson.' He flicked his eyebrows.

'All right.' She smiled, and it seemed she almost squirmed.

'How do you say love?'

She put her lips together, then released the tiny pout and said, '*Amor.*'

'How about if you want to put it in a sentence, with a couple of people?'

'I'm not sure,' she teased. 'It depends on which two people. You tell me in English, and then I'll tell you how to say it in Spanish.'

He put his arm around her and met her eyes with his. 'I love you.'

She smiled and moved her lips. Then she said, '*Tè quiero.*'

'Tay kyerro?'

'*Sí. Tè quiero. Te quiero mucho.*'

Then they moved toward each other, and he closed his eyes on the image of white dress, brown skin, gray shawl, and dark flowing hair.

CHAPTER 17

Clat watched a magpie pecking at the crust he had pared away from the underside of Rusty's hoofs. Later in the summer, the ground would be dry and the horse hoofs would be hard and brittle. It hadn't rained for a few days, but the land wasn't parched yet. Summer had come into July, or Joo-lye as Highpockets would say. The boss at the stockyards had said to come back later in the week, so Clay didn't have much to do except trim his horse's hoofs and watch the magpies.

He was camped at the river again. With the old discarded tent poles and his odd pieces of canvas, he had rigged up a ragtag shelter for his camping gear. Jackson Mead wasn't back yet, but Clay had had no difficulty picking up his few belongings. He had also rounded up his gear from the livery stable, and now he had his few things together.

A second magpie dropped down to the ground, bickering with the first one. Clay got up and walked toward them, and they both flew away. He looked at the sun slipping in the west. It was Tuesday. A couple of more days, and then maybe he could go to work.

Here came Tony Campos on his horse. He waved from a distance and flashed a smile from beneath the straw hat. Clay waved back. When Campos got to the campsite he dropped down off his horse and shook Clay's hand.

'How you doin', partner?'

'Fair enough, I suppose. Just waitin' to go to work.'

'That's what I come by about.'

'Oh?'

'Yeah. Boss got a carload of grain to unload. Be a day's work. He says if you're not busy tomorrow, be there at seven.'

'I'll be there. Work's work.'

Tony looked at the little shelter. 'You ain't got much to live in here, partner.'

'It's good enough. I'm back on my feet, anyway. As soon as I get some work I think I'll get a room, and then I'll see about getting a bunkhouse job again after a while. Like I said the other day, I've just got to build back up.'

Tony said, 'You're takin' it pretty good.'

Clay laughed. 'I've learned to. And really, there's not much they can do to me now. They can run a few cows over my land, and I won't even know it. I'm done fighting it. I'll go back out there when I'm ready to build another house and stay there.'

Tony nodded. 'When you get ready, you let me know. We'll all help. We'll have a party. Kill a pig and cook it.'

Clay laughed. 'That sounds like just the plan.'

After a day of unloading hundred-pound sacks of oats and stacking them in the warehouse, Clay had another day's work cleaning stock pens. He had the feeling that the boss was trying him out, which may have been the case. On Friday, Clay was digging postholes for the new shipping pens. It was hard work in the hot sun, but it was work.

On Saturday, as he was back at it, a few hands from the Ten Mile drifted by and stopped to talk. They said roundup was over and the Cross Pole boys were probably not long behind them. Clay told them where he was camped and that he'd probably see them later on.

Earlier in the week when he was idle, Clay had had time to wash clothes, so he had a clean shirt to wear to town on Saturday night. It would be good to see the boys again, he thought as he cleaned up in camp. They were still his friends, regardless of what had happened between him and Peck. That was, Jamie and Bill were his friends. Highpockets would probably stay at the bunkhouse anyway.

By the time he had fixed and eaten supper and tidied up camp, the sun had gone down and night was closing in. The days were still long, but they were getting shorter by a couple of minutes every day. It was dark when Clay reached Main Street. The lights were on and the music was playing in the Red Rose Saloon.

There was a crowd inside, including many men Clay had never seen before. They could not all have come off roundup. In general, the strangers were a rough-cut, working-class bunch mixed in with but distinguishable from the cowpunchers. The newcomers were of a different shade and grain, browned by a different sun and blown on by a different wind, it looked like. They wore clothes much like the locals did, but they lacked bandanas, riding boots, and spurs. Clay learned that these were the men on Sutton's ditch project – teamsters, graders, engineers, laborers. They had come to town in a trainload that day and had set up a tent camp on the other side of the river, not far from Mexican town. The next trainload was due in on Wednesday, with the rest of the equipment and men. Then the whole camp would move southwest to set up camp again, and the project would begin.

Everything was thick in the Red Rose – the mass of bodies, the smoke, the noise. Clay wormed his way through the crowd, looking for his friends. Finally he found Two-Dollar Bill, all slicked up, with his foot on the rail. When he saw Clay, Bill put his arm around Clay's shoulders, tapped his glass on the bar, and called for drinks. Then he looked at himself in the mirror and sang,

Ah'm an old lone wolf with a bob-war tail,
An' it's my night to howl!'

Clay grinned. Bill was getting underway. 'Is Jamie here?' he shouted.

'Yeah, he's somewhere.' Bill handed Clay a glass of whiskey. 'Here's to yuh!' he said, and they clacked their glasses together.

'Well, how's everything, Bill?'

'Sweet as a peach.'

'Happy to have some time off?'

'Happy about the whole shit-aree.' Then, after a whoop, he sang again,

Ah'm an old lone wolf with a bob-war tail,
An' it's my night to howl!

Clay was getting the idea.

Someone pushed up against Clay on his way to the bar. Clay turned. It was one of the newcomers. Clay turned back to Bill and shouted, 'How about the kid?'

'Mulkey wouldn't let him come. Said he was too young. He is.'

'And Slim?'

'He's here. He rode in with us.'

Clay nodded. He was jostled again and didn't bother to turn and look.

Bill raised his glass again. Clay met it. 'We missed yuh, Clay! Dammit, we missed yuh!'

'Well, I missed all of you.'

'You gotta come back, boy. You gotta come back.'

'I'd like to.'

'Don't just like to. Do it! Hey! Here's Jamie Belle!'

Jamie had worked his way through the crowd and was standing between Clay and Bill. As he shook Clay's hand he leaned forward and said loudly, 'Hell of a crowd, isn't it?'

'Sure is. How've you been?'

'Just fine. We missed you. How have you been?'

'Oh, all right.'

Jamie said, 'Let's get back out of the way where we can talk.'

'That sounds fine to me.'

Bill turned and leaned with his left elbow on the bar as Jamie and Clay took leave. Bill stuck out his hand and shook Clay's. 'Come back when you want to have another drink,' he said. Then he turned back to the bar and whooped before launching into his song again.

When they were off to the side, Clay asked Jamie, 'Where's Slim?'

'He's sitting at a table toward the back. He's just about dead drunk already.'

'How long have you been here?'

'A couple of hours.' Jamie raised his glass to meet Clay's. Then he said, 'Well, tell me how you've been gettin' by.'

'Up and down and all around. Let's see. After I saw you I built my shack. Then Sutton and Thode tried to run me off. I went to Cheyenne to check on my claim, and when I got back they'd burned my shack.'

'Really. I'd heard you had a fire, but I didn't hear the rest of it.'

'What next. Then I went and camped on the river, and I had a fight with Thode. The next day, he came back and rode into the river and drowned.'

'I heard that.'

'Then I took some tenderfeet up to the French Lakes, and someone tagged along and burned up my tent and other gear.'

'Is that right? I hadn't heard any of that.'

'It just happened last week. Now I'm back, and I'm working at the stockyards, building pens.'

'You've been busy.'

'Sometimes. How about you? What's new at the Cross Pole?'

Jamie looked at him. 'Didn't Bill tell you?'

'No. Tell me what?'

'Peck's pullin' out.'

'Really? Where to?'

'He's off to the Silver Plains. He had an offer from Sutton, and when we got back from roundup he pulled the pin on our outfit. He and the missus are packin' up right now, I imagine.'

'Sutton must have big plans.'

Jamie looked around at the crowd. 'He's got the whole ditch project ready to go.'

'That's what I heard.'

'They're scheduled to start next week. From what I understood, they're going to build a dam and reservoir out on the west end of the Courtland spread.'

'That's a ways out. Over twenty miles.'

'Then they'll cut the big ditch north and east, almost to the river.'

148

'Well, that's just dandy. I suppose he's slappin' his brand on the Courtland place, then.'

'He's supposed to join her in happy matrimony in a week or two. I'm not sure of the date. I wasn't invited.' Jamie tipped his drink.

'Neither was I.' Clay paused. Then he said, 'So Sutton's putting it all together. He tried to buy my place, but I turned him down. We even had a little fistfight over it.'

Jamie widened his eyes. 'Who won?'

'No one. I just didn't give in and sell, was what it amounted to.' Clay looked around. 'So these are all his little angels, come to dig the big ditch for him and open up the country for the punkin rollers.'

'I suppose.'

'And Peck gets a big piece of the pie. I suppose Highpockets is sore, or did he go with him?'

'No, Highpockets is here.'

'Here?'

'Yeah. He rode to town with us. He's galled about it all, and he came in to sulk.'

'Where is he? With Slim?'

'No, but he's back there. He's at a table with some of the Ten Milers.'

'Is he takin' strong drink?'

'That he is.'

'Well, I suppose I should bury the hatchet and say hello to him.'

'I imagine. Let's work our way back over to Bill and get another drink, and then we'll find Highpockets.'

Clay paused. 'By the way, I take it he didn't move up to foreman.'

'Oh, hell no. That's part of why he's put out. After all his maneuvering, they're bringing in someone new.'

'Then that's why Bill said I should come back.'

'Uh-huh. We're shorthanded, have been, and we'd all like to see you back.'

'Even Highpockets?'

'Probably even Highpockets. You know how he likes to have

peace in the family.' Jamie smiled, and the scar above his eyebrow danced.

'Yeah, I know.'

They found Two-Dollar Bill and heard him deliver his whoop and war song again. He insisted on buying a round and then toasting. 'Here's to the old hands,' he said, 'and to hell with the peckernecks!'

They drank.

When Jamie and Clay moved away through the crowd, Clay said, 'I hope you all plan to stay in town tonight.'

'We'll have to.'

They found Slim before they found Highpockets. Slim had his hat back on his head and cocked to the left side.

'Do you remember Clay?' asked Jamie.

'You bet.'

Clay shook his hand. 'How are you, Slim?'

'Drunker'n seven hunnerd dollars.'

'Good to see you.'

'You bet.' Slim's head dipped, and then he jerked it up and smiled.

When they found Highpockets, he was sitting up straight, looking sober. He had his forearms on the table, and his right hand was resting on a drink glass. Some of the older punchers from the other outfits, including the Ten Mile, were sitting around the table. Highpockets' face was nearly expressionless, with the face muscles relaxed and the mouth set straight. His eyes didn't droop, but they weren't bright either. When he saw Clay, his eyes widened slowly.

Clay said hello around to the other punchers, shaking their hands, until he came to Highpockets.

'Hello, Clay,' said the older man, looking up but otherwise not moving.

'Hello, Highpockets.' Clay put out his hand, and they shook.

'Siddown,' said Highpockets.

Clay looked around. The other punchers scooted their chairs to make room, and one of them found two chairs from farther back. Clay and Jamie sat down. Two of the men were smoking pipes, and the air was even thicker around the table than in the rest of the saloon.

Highpockets sat with his hand on his drink, his eyes dull but not glazed. Then he said, 'It's good to see you, boy.'

'Thanks. It's good to see you.' Then, after a silence of a couple of minutes, Clay said, 'I understand there have been some changes at the Cross Pole. One, anyway.'

Highpockets nodded. He rotated the drink glass about a quarter of a turn. Then he said, 'They didn't treat you right.'

'Well, I know that.' Clay thought about what hand Highpockets might have had in the treatment, and he realized that by shifting the blame, Highpockets was coming as close as he was going to come to an apology. Clay decided to take it that way and not hold a grudge. He said, 'And I thank you for saying it.'

'They did. . . .'

'They did what?' It seemed as if Highpockets had jumped a link, thinking someone had said something he hadn't.

'Sutton did you some dirt. Him an' Thode.' Highpockets' voice was slower than usual, and not as squeaky.

'I know,' said Clay.

'They had it in for you, and they did you dirt.'

'Yeah, they sure did.'

'I could tell you some things, but I won't.'

'That's all right, Highpockets. I'm not asking you to tell on anyone.' Yet he could sense that Highpockets wanted to do just that – squeal on the ones he used to squeal to. He had been their little helper, as Jamie had said, and instead of giving him a chair by the fire, they had left him out in the cold. Now he was kissing up on the other side, and Clay didn't like being a part of it. Nevertheless, it was apparent that Highpockets wanted to talk.

'It was some real dirt.'

'I know. But that's all right. I'm done with it. It's all in the past. If I can come back to the Cross Pole, fine, and if I can't, that's fine, too.'

Highpockets raised his right arm carefully and patted Clay's shoulder. 'We want you back. We'll all put in a good word for you.'

'Well, what's done is done,' said Clay, trying to draw the visit to a close.

Highpockets still had his hand on Clay's shoulder. He moved his lips, then swallowed. Then he said, 'He's not done with you yet, boy. I can tell you that much.'

Clay met eyes with the older man, giving him a questioning look. It seemed as if there was something important here.

Highpockets nodded. 'You think old Highpockets is a shitface. But I'm bein' your friend. So I'm tellin' you somethin' you didn't hear from me.'

Clay nodded.

'Sutton is gonna cut that ditch clean across your land.'

CHAPTER 18

On Sunday morning, Clay found the ditch crew's camp without any problem. What few men were up were hung over and surly, and they did not seem pleased to see a jingle-spur cowboy in their camp. After some inquiry, Clay found the head engineer's tent. The man was crouched before a folding chair in front of his tent, shaving by daylight and a small mirror. He was clear-eyed and apparently clearheaded, and he told Clay he would be with him in a few minutes.

The engineer was a tall, slender man about forty-five years old. He had graying hair slicked back from his temples and puffing out from his open-necked undershirt. When he emptied the basin and wiped the shaving soap off his face, he asked Clay what he could do for him.

Clay shook his hand. 'My name's Clay Westbrook, and I have a homestead claim out in the area where I understand you plan to run a ditch.'

'Well, good for you, Mr Westbrook. Then you stand to benefit from the irrigation that our project will bring.'

'Not from what I understand. I've been told you plan to run the ditch across my property.'

The engineer was buttoning a clean white shirt that he had put on over his undershirt. 'I don't recall any easements connected with that name.'

'Probably not. That's why I'm here.'

The engineer seemed perturbed by the remark, as if Clay had been telling him how to do his work. Clay decided to back up and try again.

'What I mean is, I think there might be a mistake. If you could show me on the map where that ditch is going to go, then I can tell you if it's my mistake or someone else's.'

The engineer took a breath, then exhaled through his nose. 'All right,' he said. 'Wait here.'

He went into the tent and came out with a metal tube. Tapping the map out of it, he said, 'This is the most recent plan.' Then he unrolled it on the roof of the tent, which came down to a side wall three feet high. 'It starts here,' he said, 'where we dam up Elk Creek. All this is the reservoir. Then the ditch comes east here. Now we see it goes up north where Saddle Creek comes in from the west. It runs parallel to Saddle Creek for almost eight miles, and then it curves to run parallel to the river, about two miles south of the river.'

'Well, this is my place here, right where you have this T. What does this T mean?'

'That's where we cut a side ditch. As I recall, it's right at a spot where there's an old burned-out homestead.'

'That's crazy,' blurted Clay, realizing that Sutton planned to carve his land into three pieces and make it useless to him.

The engineer's green-gray eyes were cold. 'Don't tell me I'm crazy. I'll roll up this map and have my men show you the way out.'

'I'm sorry,' said Clay. 'I didn't say you were crazy. I meant the plan is. That's my place, right where the T is.'

The engineer looked at him and licked his upper lip. 'Mr Sutton is contracting with us to build his ditch. We're an independent contractor. We're not working for the government. The government projects are way behind us and won't be here for a few more years, if at all. Mr Sutton makes arrangements for the land, assures us that the way is clear, and we make the dirt fly.'

'What did you mean about easements, then?'

'Mr Sutton drew our attention to those places where he didn't have title and where the landowners might be out to talk to us. But this place isn't one of them. He said he had clear title all along here.' The engineer dragged his finger across Clay's quarter section.

Clay stared at the map, eyes wide. He took a breath and phrased his remark carefully. 'It's not my mistake. I have a homestead claim on that spot, and I have papers to prove it.'

The engineer looked at him as if a little door had opened upstairs. 'Are you sure?'

'Yes, I'm sure. Very sure. I even rode to Cheyenne almost a month ago to make sure.'

'Well, that's interesting.' The engineer began to roll up the map. 'Are we done with this?'

'I am. I've said what I came to say.'

'And I thank you. I'll have to talk with Mr Sutton about this. The liability wouldn't be ours, but we could be dragged into it nevertheless. If he doesn't have clear access, and we know it, we're not cutting a ditch there.'

'Believe me, he doesn't.'

The engineer tapped the rolled-up map in his left palm. 'I'll find out.'

As Clay walked back to his horse, he sorted things through again. Sutton wanted to see Clay buckle under a dominant will. In bunkhouse terms, it was the difference between sweet-talkin' her and just takin' it. If Sutton could have cut the ditch like he planned, and ruined the parcel for Clay, the big man might have demoralized the little landowner enough to make him give in and sell after all. Now it looked as if Sutton wouldn't get things his way after all.

It was midmorning when Clay rode into town. He had told Jamie he would look for them in the café, where the Cross Pole hands would be trying to firm up Slim's and perhaps Bill's rubber legs. When Clay walked into the café, the place was packed and buzzing. He found the Cross Pole table and sat down. The four men had platters of steak and potatoes and eggs, with coffee all around. A stone-faced Highpockets said hello, as did Jamie, Bill, and glassy-eyed Slim.

'What's new?' asked Clay.

'Jackson Mead got back to town,' said Jamie.

'I knew he was gone,' Clay said, 'but I didn't know where.'

'He had a trip to make down to Rabin, down in New Mexico territory, and on the way back he made a side trip to Garden City, Kansas.'

Clay rolled his eyes up and then back down. 'Quite a little side trip.'

Jamie went on. 'He did some poking around, and he brought back a newspaper dated about a year and a half ago.'

Clay sensed that there was an interesting story about to come out. 'Uh-huh.'

'The newspaper already made it around this table – actually, I read it out loud – and now the boys from the WD are looking it over. But I can give you the gist of it.'

'Go ahead.'

'It seems our friend Sutton had a land scheme down there,' Jamie began.

'A boondoggle,' said Two-Dollar Bill.

Jamie continued, 'He did more or less what he planned to do here – line up investors, get a monopoly on a large tract of land, contract for a big irrigation project, sell land with irrigation rights—'

'And—?'

'—and the whole thing went bust, halfway through. The investors lost money, the contractor got stuck for not being able to finish the project, and the farmers got high-priced land with rights to irrigation that will never get there – not from that project anyway.'

'And Sutton?'

'He wiggled out of it and landed on his feet here, with enough money to start the Silver Plains Land and Cattle Company.'

'I would imagine this news might slow him down.' Clay looked at Highpockets, who was saying nothing.

Jamie answered. 'I'd bet so. You know how it is. When a man gets to be known as a fraud in this country, he's all done.'

Two-Dollar Bill sniffed. 'He'll get out of it, even if it all comes

155

down around him. He's probably got money stashed, and he'll go off to Idaho and start all over. It might slow him down, but it won't stop him. He'll stick it to someone else.'

Highpockets still held his quiet.

Jamie said, 'I can think of a blonde person in the widow category who might take notice.'

'This'll get out there like wildfire,' said Bill.

Clay said, 'I suppose the ditch engineer will get wind of it, too.'

Two-Dollar Bill laughed. 'I wonder what'll get to the Silver Plains first – Peck or the news.'

The boys chatted on as they finished their meal and drank more coffee. As the topic moved from Sutton to the regular chitchat, Highpockets came back into the conversation. Slim's comments were restricted to mumbles of agreement, and he kept his eyes on the table. As the boys all got up and said goodbye to the other punchers in the café, Clay got Jamie aside long enough to say, 'Next time you're in town, get a little time for yourself. I want you to meet my girl.'

Jamie looked at him wide-eyed. 'Really? How busy have you been?'

'I'll tell you all about it when we've got a few more minutes.' Then Clay shook hands with the Cross Pole boys, said so long to the others he knew in the café, and went back to his camp.

It took about a week for the news to get around the country and back into town. During that time, the Garden City newspaper drifted over to the Red Rose Saloon and rested there. For the next several days it was read aloud, silently, and in all manners in between. By the end of the week, Clay had heard that Louise Courtland was by no means going to marry Theodore Sutton of Silver Plains. On the heels of that announcement came the news that the whole ditch crew, with its two waves of men and equipment, was packing up to go back to Lincoln. As for Peck, he was at the Silver Plains just long enough to be unable to go back to the Cross Pole. The owners in St Louis were unhappy that he left on short notice in the middle of the season.

Jamie Bellefleur's pronouncement seemed to be coming true also: Sutton was known as a fraud, and he was not long for this country. He had the Silver Plains headquarters up for sale, along with the land that he actually owned.

Clay heard all of this, and it didn't bring him any pleasure. He had already decided he was done fighting with Sutton. And he knew the law was on his side, so the ditch wouldn't have gone through his place anyway. There were moments when he thought Sutton hadn't been punished enough, and he even wished he could have had more of a hand in it. Then there were other times when he thought that the disgrace and shame were punishment enough.

Clay was especially interested in knowing how Jackson Mead would see things, since the trapper had been the person who brought the news to town. Clay finally met up with him at the end of the week, on Friday.

There was a tone of satisfaction in Mead's voice as he told Clay, 'Nothing works as good as the truth, if there's some to be had, on these kind. They lie and steal and take what they want, and try to keep everyone under their thumb. Can't play square even if they wanted. That's why the truth works so well.'

'Yeah,' said Clay, 'but he'll go somewhere else and do the same thing to someone else. Like Two-Dollar Bill said, there's nothing to keep him from going across the mountains and trying it again.'

'Well,' said Mead, 'that very well could be. But the good thing is, we're rid of him here.'

'I guess so,' Clay agreed. 'We take what we get.'

Clay was still working at the stockyards during this time. He and Tony had taken to riding back and forth together. Since the day Tony had offered to roast a pig for Clay, any tension over Clay seeing his niece seemed to have gone away. Clay and Lupita weren't formally engaged, but their romance had definitely seen a turning point the day they had declared their love for one another. Clay was comfortable with the whole idea himself, and he could tell that the family was seeing things that way, too. He had come to understand that once a young couple was serious, the father (or Tony, in this case) didn't have to treat the young man so distantly. Lupita must have let her aunt and uncle know, in some discreet way, that she and Clay were serious. Looking back, Clay understood that Tony's offer to cook a pig was his way of recognizing what hadn't yet been officially declared.

On Saturday, after they had worked late, with Tony helping Clay finish hanging a gate, they rode to Clay's camp. Although the sun was going down, Tony seemed in no more of a hurry than usual. He stayed around to chat as Clay put Rusty out to graze and started to build his evening fire.

The sound of horses crossing the river caused Clay to stand up and turn around. At the same time, Tony stepped back away from the fire and stood at Clay's left.

Dusk was gathering, and it was even thicker off in the trees by the river. Clay watched closely. It looked as if two men on horseback were hanging back in the trees as one man rode forward. It was a large shape, the horse and rider coming his way. The scuff of hoofs carried on the evening air. Clay looked at Tony, who nodded back.

As the rider came closer, Clay was not surprised to see that it was Sutton. The man stopped his horse thirty yards from the campfire but did not get down.

'I came to see you, Westbrook.'

'So it seems.'

There was a moment of silence, with just the small flame whispering in the firepit, until Sutton spoke back. 'I came to settle things.'

'I don't know what there is to settle. I'm keeping my land, and that's it.'

'You know that's not why I came. I can't use that land now. You saw to that, you and your snivelin' friends.'

'How?'

'You and that squaw-man Mead. Got no shame at all, wantin' to ruin a man's name, spreadin' rumors.'

Clay couldn't tell if Sutton really thought he had helped spread the news about the fraud. Maybe Sutton was just trying to push him into a fight. Clay felt calm as he answered back, using some of Jackson Mead's language. 'The truth is the truth, Sutton, and it sounds like it hurts.'

'Don't crow to me, you little bastard.'

'I'm not crowing. I'm not the one who brought back that news and let it out, but if I'd been in his place, I'd have done the same thing.'

Sutton was quiet for a long moment. Then he said, 'I came here to have it out with you, once and for all, but I didn't expect to see your little Mexican friend here.'

'Neither did Mack.'

'What's that supposed to mean?'

'Nothing if you don't already know. But I'm not going to fight you, Sutton. I've already decided that. And I'm not letting you have the satisfaction of pushing me into it.'

'Sounds like you've lost your nerve, you little tramp.'

'Nope. You just don't get things your way, that's all.'

It had gotten darker in just those few minutes, and when Clay saw motion he thought Sutton might be bringing out a gun. To the contrary, he was gathering his reins. He swore at the two men, then turned his horse around and rode off into the dusk toward the river. Clay heard a voice, the shuffling of hoofs, and then the sound of horses crossing the river and climbing the other bank.

Clay turned and said to Tony, 'I'm glad you were here for that.'

Tony's smile flashed in the firelight. 'Me too. That was better than knockin' him on his ass.' He turned down the corners of his mouth. 'Maybe.'

The next day, as Clay and Lupita stood on the bluff overlooking the river, he told her about the latest developments. He was happy to be able to tell her that his recent troubles were all in the past.

Toward the end of his story he said, 'On one hand, I think he should have been punished more. But on the other, I'm satisfied with what happened. I want no part of carrying a grudge and wishing more grief on him.'

Lupita agreed. 'That's a good way to look at it.' Then she added her view of the subject. 'We say, *Dios castiga.* God punishes.'

Clay thought about that for a moment. It seemed like a good idea, too. He knew, as he knew Lupita knew, that they could both be right at a time like this. They could see it from their slightly different points of view, and they could have an understanding that included both.

Tony and Margarita had climbed the bluff with them that day. The chaperones had politely walked away for a few minutes, with their backs turned. Clay took advantage of the moment to put his arm around Lupita.

He looked off to the west and said, 'Up in those mountains, there's a beautiful place I'd like to show you someday. I've wanted to take you there since the day I saw it with those two tenderfeet. All I could think of was you. I thought we should be there together. There are canyons, lakes, forests – you'll have to see it for yourself.' He looked into her eyes. 'Someday when we don't need a chaperone any more.'

'I'd like to see it,' she said, her eyes glistening.

Their lips met and a single current was formed between them.